Perspective

Inspired by a True Story

Mallory Kotzman

BALBOA.PRESS
A DIVISION OF HAY HOUSE

Balboa Press books may be ordered through booksellers or by contacting:

Balboa Press
A Division of Hay House
1663 Liberty Drive
Bloomington, IN 47403
www.balboapress.com
844-682-1282

Print information available on the last page.

ISBN: 978-1-9822-7669-0 (sc)
ISBN: 978-1-9822-7671-3 (hc)
ISBN: 978-1-9822-7670-6 (e)

Library of Congress Control Number: 2021923149

Balboa Press rev. date: 11/17/2021

For the Mallory I have been. For the Mallory I have yet to be.
For anyone that is living with grief – and all that comes with it.
This is for you.

Introduction

This isn't going to be a book for everyone. Some of you may hate it. Some of you may love it. Some of you may take it or leave it. Some of you may think that Emerson is a whiny girl who needs to get over it. Some of you may pity her. To be honest with you, I don't care. I didn't write it for you.

I wrote this book for me. I needed to write it, even though I didn't want to. I had been working on another novel for a long time; a novel that had nothing to do shame or depression or fear. But here we are, all because of a meditation.

I have meditated for years as a way to quiet the incessant chatter that is my mind. When I moved to New York, my meditations became something else entirely – taking on a life of their own. And in April of 2020 I had the most vivid one I'd ever had. I was catapulted into a scene that was so real to me, I could taste it. I could feel the air. I could feel the texture of what I was wearing. I could feel myself. And when I came out of that meditation, my face wet with the tears of incandescent joy, I heard something. I heard a voice that didn't belong to me, but it was a voice I inherently knew. It was loving. It was supportive. It was familiar even though I'd never consciously heard it before. I knew it was God. And God told me, "It's not the novel."

I didn't want to listen. I didn't want to believe that God had a message or a plan for me - especially one that so clearly didn't coincide with the plan I had for myself. I really didn't want to write a book like this. I wanted to write the novel I'd been writing - a lovely, magical, fictional novel that had nothing to do with anything real. I wanted to escape emotional reality, not dive further into it.

So, I ignored that voice. I did research on the fun novel. I sketched out apartment layouts for the main characters. I wrote scenes that were almost good, but not quite. And somehow, each time I placed pen to paper, or my hands upon the keys of my laptop, I knew that I was just prolonging the inevitable.

I don't know if you've ever fought with God. I don't know if you've ever had Them come to you when you're open and willing and throw a wrench in your plans. I have. I really didn't want to write this book. Personally, I am all too familiar with grief and loss. And there is something I know to be true: Grief doesn't ever go away. It evolves as your life evolves. The sharp pain of losing someone you love and their sudden absence from the world in the beginning is very different than the realization that ten years later they would be an age you couldn't possibly fathom them growing into. That you can't call them up and invite them to a home they've never been to, to see you in a life they won't get.

Even more difficult than writing about something so intimately personal, came the quandary of how I could illustrate the complexity of mourning relationships that were mentally, emotionally, and even physically abusive. I've read a great many books while searching for answers. Books on how to forgive. How to be angry. How to live your life after someone dies. How to live your life after abuse. But I've never read a book that told me that it was okay to still love those abusers, or how to mourn them without shame. I realized that I wanted permission to do just that. And it occurred to me that I was the only one who could give permission to myself. And that maybe - just maybe - I might not be the only one who needed it.

So, after a long, arduous fight with God, I wrote a book. I don't have to tell you what happens when you fight with God, but this is the book. And it's not that novel.

Fall

*October's poplars are flaming torches lighting
the way to winter.* – Nova S. Blair

Loss

Death ends a life, not a relationship. – Mitch Albom

W e weren't a close-knit family. We weren't a functional family. But we were a family. Until we weren't. We were a family that died and a family that left. And then we, became me.

The day that I knew it would become just me, I stood in the doorway of a hospital room in a town I'd never been to. The last of my family lay on the bed before me, bloated and unrecognizable. The machines keeping him alive were almost louder than the blood in my ears. Almost.

In front of me was the last person in the world I shared parents with; the last person I shared trauma with, the last person I shared childhood Christmases with. He and I had the same nose, the same eyes, and the same longing for acceptance. He was my brother, Keating. And the battle that he'd fought for as long as I could remember, was finally lost.

There was a presence to my left, just inside the doorway pulling me in. I knew who it was. We'd met so many times before. I knew her energy as well as I knew the scar on the back of my right hand.

"Hello, Loss."

She didn't respond. She didn't have to. The machines were pumping his blood, breathing for him, keeping him in a medically induced coma to give his body time to heal. But I knew he wasn't there, in that body. Not anymore.

When I walked into the room, his heart rate spiked. He knew I was here. I knew he was still here somewhere. I could feel him. I could feel him the way I could feel Loss – heavy, expectant, waiting. When I turned to my left, I could almost see him there in the shadows, resplendent in a chair that he'd brought in himself, unhappy with the hospital decor. It would probably be a burnished leather, and he would likely be swirling a glass of obscenely expensive red wine. He would have crossed his legs, displaying the bright pink of his sock that was so perfect with his exquisitely tailored, bespoke suit. His hair would be floppy from running his hands through it, and his nails would be manicured. His glasses thick, classy, with the faintest hint of trend.

As I imagined this, I became divided – part of me flew into the room asking questions, absorbing any bit of information like a sponge. The other sat by his side, clutching a hand that was colder than typical, but not quite gone. When I looked up, I saw one brittle string tethering his spirit to his body. He *was* in the room. But the vision I saw in the suit wasn't my brother.

"You're not surprised to see me, Emerson." His words slid into my mind like smoke from a bonfire; pungently compelling.

"No." I watched as my body sat in a chair next to the hospital bed, arms wrapped around myself unconsciously trying to keep warm against the chill. After what seemed like hours with the figure watching me from across the room, my shock finally wore off. And I was left alone with the body of what was left of my brother and the energy across the room that was almost his.

"I know who you are."

There was the faintest hint of smile in his tight lips. "I know you do."

Loss held my hand. She was quietly insistent, and though I knew it wouldn't last long, I ignored her.

"You're very beautiful." My voice is barely a whisper. "I didn't expect you to be, but you are."

"Am I?" The figure shrugged elegantly. "Everyone sees me differently."

Looking around the room, I note a distinct lack of personal effects. "What happened?"

Loss chooses this moment to communicate. She brings in the nurses, the doctors, the police. One of the nurses tells me that they've been trying to find me. Before I can respond to her, the police come in. They explain to me that Keating had created quite the scene in his hotel room. He screamed. He threw things. He made unimaginable demands, and finally not knowing what to do, the front desk had called 911. One of the police coaxed him into an ambulance. While he was on his way to the hospital where I now sat, still another searched his room. They found an alarming variety of drugs and alcohol out in the open.

When he arrived at the hospital, he was still screaming, but the nurses told me through pitying eyes that he was sobbing as well. I could see it. I could see my erratic, emotional brother, looming over these delicate nurses, screaming through his tears. One nurse told me that he kept saying the same thing over and over, until the drugs finally caused him to pass out and slip into a coma.

"What was it that he kept saying?"

She doesn't want to look at me while she answers my question, pity evident in her eyes.

"It's okay," I reassure her. "I'd like to know."

After chewing on her lower lip, she finally whispers, "I'm so lonely."

My head nods even as my heart breaks.

"Thank you."

She takes it as dismissal. I fall back into the chair, bemoaning the lack of comfort in hospital furniture, and both of my hands are gripped in silent reminder. One is held by Loss, who hasn't let go since I got to the hospital. The other by my husband, Taggart who drove us from Ohio straight through to Illinois without stopping.

Neither say anything. My eyes are locked on the image across the room.

"What really happened?"

There is no doubt who this question is for.

The figure sets down the goblet of wine on a nearby table. He takes off his glasses and rubs the bridge of his nose.

"I know who you are," I repeat.

"Yes, I know you, too. I'm very familiar with your family. Though I must say, I didn't expect for us to meet quite like this."

"Is there anything I can do to stop you?"

The figure hesitates, and I feel a sweeping moment of sympathy. "No, Emerson. It's not up to you."

Sighing deeply, I accept this. "I just had to ask. How much time is left?"

He checks his left wrist. "Physically? About a week. Mentally? I'm afraid it's too late."

Nodding in understanding, I repeat my earlier question.

"What really happened?"

The figure I know to be Death raises his eyes to mine. We stare silently at one another until I hear the truth in his answer.

"He asked for me, Emerson."

I run out of the room Loss hot on my heels. Finding a bathroom, I usher her in and lock the door. She holds my hair back as I vomit until there is nothing left but the gaping hole I know she is responsible for. I yell at her. I try to throw her out of my life for something like the millionth time, but she's strong. So strong that she holds onto me while I cry on yet another bathroom floor, wailing until I almost black out from the pain.

"Why, Loss? *Why?*" I sob against her chest, so familiar to me now it almost smells like home. "Why are you such a big part of my life?"

I stare at Loss; immovable and inveterate as ever. I know her so well. She's watched me grow up, and in the last few years has been even more tangible than ever.

Just as I am getting back on my feet, here she comes barreling in yet again. Deep down, I had always known Death would come for Keating. I knew it would happen sooner or later, and I am as prepared for that as I can possibly be. What I'm not prepared for is what this staggering loss of my brother means. It means there will be no more brothers to reach out to during the holidays. It means there will never again be anyone to share in childhood memories with. That connection we shared, however distant and flimsy, will be snapped, and this final Loss will be the end of the family I grew up with.

It will be the end of those brilliantly complex strings that held our family together. There will be no more fights. No more boundaries ignored. No more hugs. No more Christmas mornings. No more us. I am completely untethered, floating in s sea of memory. There is but one lone string connecting me to my husband. For that string I am so, so grateful. But that one string — the sole string I had left? What if Loss took that, too?

Leaning against the bathroom door, I hear Loss apologizing. It was her job, she said. She doesn't make the rules, only carries out orders. She's sobbing too. She knows what this means for me, and as she cries, each tear that falls from her eyes is a memory of what she has taken.

I feel like Alice in Wonderland drowning in her tears, and soon, I am surrounded by what I've lost. The sheer depth and volume of it is taking me by surprise. I'm treading water, but barely. Loss has never done this before. Usually she's quiet, though present. She has become like my shadow over the years; just another thing I ignored and took for granted as a way of life. I've long since stopped fighting her. And here, in this hospital, in one fell swoop she took not only my brother, but my family, and all the potential shared memories that went with it.

A wave came in, seemingly impossible in this small space, but it came all the same. It takes me under, my limbs flailing. And with every saltwater burn of my eyes, I remember.

I remember a twilight September evening, driving home when Loss called me. Loss told me that Death had come for my father, Calvin. It was my first real encounter with Death, though he hadn't shown himself to me directly yet. The details were fuzzy with shock, but it was clear my father had been found alone.

Loss takes me back to that moment while I'm under the wave. I'm not merely remembering. I am reliving. I am reliving the moment the first realizations of my life had taken place. Loss had already taken my father from me, but he'd always been out there – this possibility that loved me more than I was ever told.

In my mind, I'm back in that car, confused because I don't know if I'm actually allowed to feel anything.

Loss's grip is strong as she holds me under. "Remember."

Suddenly, inexplicably, in this moment with her, under the wave of memory, I am a little girl again. And that little girl in me remembers how my father had smelled like Old Spice and loved Reese's peanut butter cups. She remembers the way he would toss her in the air and catch her. The way his whiskers scratched her when he kissed her. The way his naval uniform always felt so stiff under her grubby fingers. That little girl remembered all the things I had been forced to forget. She remembers things I wasn't allowed to remember without hurting my mother or the man my mother had said was our father now. In the water, I watch the blurry memory slip away.

In its place, is the loss of the family I had known. The beginning of the loss of my brother, Keating — the one who lay in the hospital room fifty feet away. And the loss of a huge chunk of both his and my identities, only to be found later in an emergency search and rescue. It was the beginning of the loss of my mother as well, but I wouldn't discover that until later.

The same week that my father died, my mother Kate was diagnosed with advanced lung cancer. This set off a chain of events that would forever alter our lives.

Just as Loss had come to take my father and the family I had known as a young child, she did it again. She did it again with disease and showed the truth of what my family was.

"Did you really lose anything, Emerson, if I just revealed what always was?" Loss sips a drink, her lazy floating contrasting with her pleading tone.

"I thought losing my mom would bring us all closer together," I say through numb lips.

Loss laughs - a sound filled with both sympathy and derision.

Three months after my mother's diagnosis; after multiple surgeries, rounds of radiation and chemotherapy; in the middle of the night the call that I had been dreading came. Death had taken her, too.

"We'd all been expecting it," came my voice through chattering teeth. "But it shook us all so hard. "

Loss fiddled with her straw. "I know. I was there for that, too. It's one of those times I wish I hadn't had to be, but the assignment is the assignment."

I try to yell at her but like me, my energy is flailing.

"Tell me what happened next, Emerson. Remind me." Her eyes lock on mine, and the wave that takes me under, goes inside me, too. It rolls in my stomach, creating the familiar place where Loss would often curl up.

My tears mix with the water and soon, I become the water. I am drowning myself in Loss, becoming one with her. And she knows it.

"You'd come for my relationship with my mom, long before she died. I would see glimpses of her true self peeking through, but then just as quickly, you'd snatch her up. Sometimes it seemed like you'd be gone, and we would make progress. But then you would pop in, making a sudden appearance and you took it - the possibility, the potential, the support. You took it all."

"Yes."

"It seemed liked we had finally gotten to a place where we could forget about you. She seemed like herself – the woman I knew she really was. We had the conversation we'd always needed to have. I finally had the understanding I'd always needed – the answers to my questions, the resolution to a lifetime of complexity. We began to have the sort of relationship we'd both longed for. The kind where I could call her up for a recipe or meet her for lunch. For a brief shining moment, we were just a mother and daughter who had been through some shit but came out the other side." My voice sounds foreign, desensitized, even to my own ears. I'm reading from a script that I already know the ending to.

"You were. You did."

"You came then, and you took her. You took the woman I knew, the woman she wanted to be, the family she held together. You didn't just take her, Loss. You took all of us when you let Death take her." Tears fall from my glazed eyes, uniting us even further.

Loss isn't floating anymore. She is in the ocean of memories with me, clutching my arms, making it harder to keep my head above water.

"I had to, Emerson. It was one of the worst parts of my job."

With no emotion in my voice, I reminded her. I reminded her how she came for my family, individually and collectively. She found my older brother, Keating, already broken, and only added to it. She took my stepfather Percy, but he wouldn't acknowledge her, and thrust her in my direction instead.

"But most of all…" this is where I stop being able to breathe. I gulp water, thinking it's air. Loss fully embraces me. She holds me for a long time in the water. I can't tell if I'm sinking or rising. It doesn't matter. I've stopped caring.

"Charles, Emerson. I took Charles."

Charles. I still couldn't say his name without wanting to cry. How do I begin to describe Charles? Charles was the brother that came when I was seven years old. He was the result of my mother and stepfather, Percy. Charles was, in a word, perfect. He was blonde haired, blue eyed, and beautiful. The most beautiful thing I'd ever seen – before or since. His heart was pure, his light was bright, and his soul was joy. He gave the greatest hugs. He had the best laugh and would shower it on anyone who was within five feet. He would do anything for anyone.

"I helped raise him, Loss."

"Yes, I remember. That was when I came for your childhood. You gave it so freely, dear." She hugs me tighter.

"You wanted Charles's childhood. I couldn't let him give his. He was just a little boy."

Memories flood me. Making him dinner while our mother was working overtime to pay the bills. Letting him teach me how to skateboard. Helping him with his homework. Signing our mother's signature on permission slips. Sneaking him to visit me when I moved out because he wasn't allowed to see me. Answering calls from him at one in the morning because he needed someone to talk to. Persuading my dates and friends to take him to his basketball practices so that he could still play. Teaching him about girls and music. Picking him up from school, singing at the top of our lungs with the windows down. Letting him steal my sunglasses. Screaming for him when he graduated high school because I had never been so proud. The dimples when he smiled. That charming, chipped front tooth, and how it added to his smile, rather than detracting from it. Him telling me he knew Taggart was the person I'd marry.

I melted into Loss. She feels so solid now, so real.

"Why him? Why us?"

She sighed then. "I don't expect you to understand. I don't know if you can. I only know that it was the assignment."

I weep into her shoulder. "It was your assignment to take everything wonderful about this boy…and he was exactly that, Loss. A boy. It was your 'assignment' to take everything from him? To take his judgment? His sense of self?"

Loss has the good sense to look resigned, as she repeats herself. "I don't expect you to understand."

"You had to know. You had to know what would happen."

Submerged again, I am taken back. Taken back to the day I was jolted out of sleep by the ringing of my phone. On the other end was my stepfather's mother, telling me that Death had come for Charles, just two months after taking my mother.

I had gone to Percy's house where Charles had still lived. There I found Percy's best friend, his parents, and his new fiancée and her daughter, both of which I'd had yet to meet. I was the last one to arrive. Bombarded with memories and emotions, I retreated to the bathroom Charles, Keating and I had once shared to collect myself.

I was responsible for calling Keating to tell him. He lived across the country and when Keating came into town we went for a long drive. Loss had been a palpable presence in the car with us, taking up all the space. Neither of us felt the need to speak. We didn't know what to say. It reminded us both how we had gone for a long drive after Mom had died as well, but Charles had been with us. This time there was no Charles. There would never be any Charles again.

"Charles was the best of us," Keating had said, choking back tears at the funeral. "Charles was my best friend."

There were a few months when it seemed everything would be alright. Percy took me to lunch for my birthday; something he'd never done. He and I talked on the phone. We spent time just the two of us, talking about Mom. Talking about Charles. Talking about his new fiancée and their upcoming wedding. But then — suddenly, surprisingly — Loss showed up. She came without Death, taking the family that I had grown up with for the past twenty years; the father I had known, the grandparents I had celebrated every holiday with, the extended cousins and aunts and uncles. She took them all without a second thought as I cried on the floor of yet another bathroom, having the last conversation I would ever have with the only father I was allowed to love.

Keating and I were on our own, but he was still living across the country and he was suffering. His own relationship between Loss and his sense of self had always been a toxic one. There were times when we could talk, and Loss wasn't present. Times I could see the brother I knew; times when we could laugh, and I could make sense of his words. These times were fleeting, and slowly, almost like magic, they disappeared.

Loss came for Keating in earnest. He still breathed. He still existed. But only just. He wasn't living, he was surviving. Loss came for my relationship with him as well. He began to talk in riddles, one minute loving and reminiscent, the next filled with rancor and blame directed at me.

"It was your job to take care of Charles!" He loved to say to me. "Why didn't you do your job? Who do you even think you are? Just some fat girl from a white trash town who won't amount to anything. You'll never be anything. You can't even take care of yourself. I should've known you wouldn't be able to take care of Mom. Or Charles. This is all your fault. If you had just taken care of them, they'd still be here. I hate you. I hate you for being so fucking selfish."

They were so similar to the last words that Percy had said to me. Only this time they were Keating's.

I had a conversation with Loss then, the first one that I instigated. I told Loss I finally understood that I needed to give her my relationship with Keating, but I needed a window — just in case. I didn't want to give it to her completely, but I would if it was what was best – for me, for my marriage, for my mental health. We agreed to a partnership, but she remained the majority owner.

This is why I wasn't surprised to see her here, at this hospital in this small town in the middle of nowhere. This is why I knew she would be here, waiting for me. This is why I locked her in the bathroom with me, afraid to let her touch my husband, my marriage.

"I don't want those things, Emerson."

"How do I know that Loss? How do I know what you want and what you don't want? You show up when I've just gotten comfortable – when I don't see you coming. I mean, just look around!" I wave arms which have become heavy. Too heavy.

She waits expectantly. She knows this has been a long time coming.

"You've taken my relationship with my father and my relationship with my mother when both of them were still alive. Then when you let Death come, you took away any possibility I had of repairing either of those relationships. You took Charles…" my voice breaks here as it always does when I speak of him. "No. You let Death take Charles. He didn't do anything to deserve that. You took my family — the only family I knew. You took Keating. I saw it. I knew you'd been with him for a long time, but he fought you. He fought you so hard, Loss. And there were times where it really seemed like he won."

I'm quiet for a moment and I know I have to address something else.

"You took me, Loss. You convinced me that my family didn't want me, that we needed space from each other."

"You did need space, Emerson. I was trying to help you ..."

I cut across her excuses, acid in my voice. "You were trying to help me? You took my sense of self, my self-respect. You weaponized everything. You made me lose who I was."

"I remember," She spoke quietly. "I didn't think you did."

The water that we were in started to roil then, lightly, making me queasy. A flash of a man who had claimed to love me flitted across my memory. He struck me, in the face, in the stomach. He told me I deserved it and I believed him. He pointed out terrible things about me and I believed them, too.

"I do. But I won that time, didn't I? It took a long time to heal from that, but I did it. I beat you. And if you try to come for my husband, my marriage, my self? I'll fight you with everything I have. And I'll win again."

I glared at her and let the waves wash over me.

"You won't take me. I won't let you."

Loss smiled for the first time. A smile of acceptance, of surrender. "Good."

Shame

Shame corrodes the very part of us that believes
we are capable of change. – Brené Brown

L oss takes her leave, and while I'm waiting for her inevitable return, I notice something lurking. It doesn't feel like Loss. I know how she works. This feels a bit voyeuristic.

Looking over my shoulder, I feel it looming. Panic rises, bile in my throat, and my gut wrenches. I think I might be sick.

A familiar figure comes into view, standing in front of my exit. He's tall, too tall, blocking the doorway but not completely. He likes to give the illusion of escape.

Something pulls me toward him. It's slippery, slick. Words form through the metallic taste in my mouth.

"Hello, Shame."

He reaches out, rubbing my shoulders too hard for comfort, his hot breath asking if I'm ready. I'm not. I never am. I know what's coming next.

His hands, sharp nails, long fingers, guide me to a seat.

"Comfy?"

As if I could ever relax with him around.

Holding my head in place, he says, "Play the film."

I hate this movie. I've seen it so many times and it always ends the same way. I try not to cry. My tears only make him stronger. I try to push away, but I'm no match for the vice my neck is in. My stomach recoils, and I want to vomit, but he plucks greasy, burnt popcorn from the bucket in my lap, forcing it through my lips.

"Watch." He whispers insidiously, making my skin crawl.

I keep my eyes open. If I don't, he'll just hold them open. Shame's done it before.

The previews start and I get sucked in like always. It's compelling, this story. I can relate to the girl on the screen. She just wants to be loved; I think. We all just want to be loved.

The girl closes her eyes as blows rain down on her brother. At the sound of guttural sobs, her eyes pop open. She looks at her mother in disbelief. Together they watch as the man throws pots and pans at the boy curled up in a protective ball on the ground.

"*Do* something!" I implore the daughter, the mother, yelling at the screen. Shame laughs. He loves it when I yell at the screen.

I have a thousand moments like these. A thousand of these movies that play in my head, and every subject of them dead save for one. The villain in the movies? It's always me.

"Talk to me," Shame invites. "Tell me."

Unable to resist, I begin.

"When Keating and Percy would fight, I did nothing. I just watched it happen. I knew better than to intervene. I knew that Percy liked me better than Keating. He told me so. He said how sweet I was, how I welcomed him into the family right away even as Keating was standoffish and awkward. He said he liked being my dad.

"Percy's friends were around a lot. They were nice to me. I was young. I was blonde. I was thin. I was malleable. They would make fun of Keating, who spent time in his room on the computer he purchased from saving his lunch money. I didn't join in, but I didn't stop them. I laughed along with them. I wanted to be included," my words trail off.

"Why did you want to be included, Emerson?" Shame strokes a finger down my cheek.

"If I could make them laugh, I could make them like me. And if they liked me, maybe I could make them love me."

My words come out in a whisper, my shoulders hunching.

"You and Keating were friends." He lights a cigarette. "Until you weren't. You were loved, until you spoke up. Let's see what happens when that changed. Let's watch."

The movie always starts out innocently.

A little girl is playing with her brother outside. It's Keating. They're close enough in height that they could be twins. They walk around holding hands. They chase their dog. They giggle when their parents tickle them. The girl's brother crawls into her bed when she has bad dreams. They fall asleep snuggling. Then things shift...

They're older now, playing in their shared bedroom. They make up games; the floor is lava; the girl's art case is a laptop and she's a business lady from another planet. Keating builds her Barbie dream house for her. He wants to be an architect. Or an astronaut.

The girl and Keating aren't allowed to call their dad 'Dad' anymore. Their mom Kate says they have to call him 'Calvin' because that's his name. She tells them if Calvin really loved them, he'd be around. Now her husband Percy is their dad. Percy doesn't have to take care of them, but he does. He doesn't have to love them, but he does. Percy stands silently, his hand heavy on their mother's shoulder.

Keating and the girl go by Percy's last name in school now even though it's not really theirs. Calvin calls and they cry. They miss Calvin. Calvin misses them. Keating cries a lot and slips up. He calls him Dad on the phone. Percy overhears and hands Keating's mom a wooden spoon. Kate cries as she spanks her son with the spoon. Keating screams. He's only ten. It hurts. The girl watches fearfully as Percy tells Keating to be quiet. Kate drops the spoon on the ground and is now holding her son. Percy picks it up, and wrenches Keating out of his mother's arms. He spanks Keating until the spoon breaks. Keating has peed his pants. Percy calls him a fairy and sends him to his room.

Keating and the girl walk two miles to and from the bus stop every day. They talk nicely to each other when no one is around. They laugh. Keating teaches her Spanish by asking her to quiz him. The girl likes words. She tells him she wants to be an artist. Or a writer. Or a translator. She tells Keating she was accepted to an art school. Keating tells her not to tell their parents. The girl doesn't listen to her brother and tells their parents. She is grounded and her art supplies are taken away. Percy and Kate go through her room and find her journals. They read them out loud in front of all their friends. The girl has written that she has a crush on the boy who lives at the end of the road. He's nice and he has beautiful dark skin. Percy doesn't like people with darker skin. He tells her she isn't allowed to be friends with him. Kate and Percy take away her notebooks and the door to her room. She doesn't have privacy anymore. Charles sits outside the doorway passing her tissues as she cries. He isn't allowed to go in. He's six.

Now they're older. Keating and the girl don't hold hands anymore. The girl laughs when the parents laugh. She jumps up to get beer for her dad and his friends. She's happy to be included. They laugh and call her their pretty little beer wench. She wears the bikini tops that her mother bought her, but she doesn't eat much. Both Percy and Kate say she's fat. She's thirteen.

Percy comes up behind her in the kitchen and grabs her butt. The girl freezes. She turns around slowly, scared and shocked. The air is filled with awkward silence. Percy says he thought the girl was Kate. They laugh it off and he walks away. The girl pushes it deep, deep down. She doesn't let herself think about the fact that her hair is bright blonde and her mother's is dark brown.

Keating is a teenager, and very smart. He likes computers and he has acne. He's very tall and when Percy isn't around Kate tells Keating how much he looks like Calvin. Keating and Percy get into an argument. Percy hits Keating until Keating is curled on the ground just outside the girl's room. She still doesn't have a door. She sees everything. Keating's eyes are squeezed shut. Percy is calling him a mean name that means he likes boys. Keating does like boys, but he isn't allowed to. His arms cover his head as a cast iron skillet barely misses his face. Charles, their younger brother, rushes toward Keating to try to help. Kate pulls him away. More pots and pans fall, in near perfect sync with insults. Keating is sobbing and apologizing. He doesn't want to like boys. He won't like them anymore. When Percy is done, their mother makes Keating pack a bag. He has to go live with Calvin. She's told them that Calvin does drugs and hates them. She makes Keating say goodbye to both Charles and the girl. When they leave, Percy watches television while he drinks beer after beer. The girl and Charles hold each other on the stairs. Charles is eight. Hours later, Keating and Kate come home. They don't say anything. Keating goes to bed.

The girl is sixteen. She has a boyfriend. Percy and her mother want to go a private campout where you have to be twenty-one to get in. They want the girl to come. Her mom tells her to wear her smallest bikini top and shortest shorts and they'll let her in. She gets in. A man asks her to dance. He's thirty-six – only one year younger than Percy. The girl is drunk, so she dances. The man asks her for her phone number. She says that she is only sixteen and has a boyfriend. He laughs and tells her that doesn't matter. The girl tells her mom. The girl laughs drunkenly as her mom writes down their phone number.

The girl is seventeen. She comes home from a date with her longtime boyfriend. She's home before curfew. She says goodnight to her parents and goes to bed. The next day her mom asks her if she's ever had sex. The girl hesitates and says she has. Kate is insulted that the girl didn't tell her. She thought they were best friends. Percy overhears. He tells the girl she's a fat whore. He spits at her, and it lands on her face. He slaps her. When they sit down to dinner, he spits in her food. He makes her eat it. He tells her if she throws it up, she'll have to eat that, too. She doesn't throw it up, but she wants to.

The girl is nineteen. Her financial aid was canceled so she left college. She has a fight with Percy and Kate about this and moves out. Now she lives with her new boyfriend and his parents. Her new boyfriend doesn't like when she wears red. He says it makes her look like a whore and throws away everything red in her closet. He weighs her every morning and every night. He makes her run laps while he times her. If she gains weight or makes him mad, he hurts her. He tells her no one else will want her. He tells her no one else will love her. She wears long sleeves in the summer and always has peas in the freezer.

The girl is twenty. She flies to Arizona to visit Calvin on her own. She hasn't seen him in eleven years. Calvin cries when he sees her at the airport and tells her how he's always loved her. He tells her how she's always been his little girl. He tells her how much she looks like her mother. The girl is uncomfortable. She tells Calvin that she needs time to adjust. She says that she may have always been his daughter, but he wasn't always her father.

The girl is twenty-five. Her mother has cancer. Percy and Charles go to visit and offer to pick the girl up. Kate is swollen with disease and muscle atrophy. The girl sits next to her bed and holds her hand. Her mother calls her 'Pumpkin' and asks how she's doing. Before the girl can answer, Percy comes into the room. They all sit and visit, but Kate lapses into sleep. Charles is quiet. When Kate wakes up, aware and alert, Percy says it's time to go. The girl stops rubbing her mother's feet to kiss her check and tell her that she loves her. Kate frantically clutches the girl's hand. There is pleading in her voice as she asks, 'Why can't Emerson stay?' Percy says they have to go and pries their hands apart even though both Kate and Emerson are crying. This is the last time the girl will see her mother.

The girl's mother has died. Charles calls her and asks her if he can come over. The girl works nights and tells him she has to take a nap before work. Charles says he doesn't care. He says he just wants to be with her. The girl takes a nap on the couch in her living room while Charles sits in a reclining chair. The girl's alarm goes off after two hours. She wakes up and asks Charles if he wants to talk. He says no and waits to leave until she leaves. At their cars, she hugs him. She tells him she loves him. He tells her he loves her, too. This is the last time the girl will see Charles.

"Stop." I demand, the words breaking. "Please. I can't."

Shame fast forwards through the rest. I know there's more. Shame has an endless supply. He gleefully looks at my tearstained face, my butter slicked lips, my swollen eyes. He feels strong. He knows he's about to get stronger. He's saved this for last.

"You still love him." He says pityingly.

I don't have to lift my eyes. I don't have to ask who. I know he means Percy. I know he knows some of my deepest Shame is that Keating killed himself because he couldn't love himself. Keating was taught to be ashamed of who he was. If he couldn't love himself, how could he ever love someone who looked like him?

"I didn't stand up for him."

Shame leans back and sucks in a breath. This is his favorite part. The spiral.

"No. You didn't."

"The girl," I choke out. "It was me."

"Yes," He encourages.

"She just – let it all happen. She knew it was wrong. Yet, she just wanted to be loved. She still loves him. She still loves him more than the father that wanted her…" I begin to sob.

"And…."

"I blame him for Keating. I blame him for Charles. But mostly. Oh God…." My shoulders hunch, my hands cover my face as tears and snot spray through my fingers.

"Say it, Emerson."

Shame's voice is firm. The pressure on my neck is back. He puts a pint of ice cream in my hand and spoon-feeds me.

My mouth automatically opens, the sweet flavor contrasting with the bitter words that I hold in my heart, in my throat, in my stomach. I swallow the ice cream and spit out the words.

"I blame myself. I should've spoken up. I should've stopped it. I just wanted to be loved. How pathetic is that? I just wanted to be loved by a man who didn't know how to love me. Or how to love anyone who didn't fit into his world? How can I still love that person knowing what they're capable of? How can I still miss them? How can I have as hard a time grieving them as I do grieving almost anyone else? How is this so painful and muddy? What if I had done something? How can I still love a person who treated so many people so horribly? And what happened behind the scenes? How could I have missed that growing up? How could I have missed all the signs that he was hurting my mother? I thought he *wanted* to love her. And me. I thought he *wanted* to be in our lives. And my father, Calvin. Calvin wanted so desperately to be in my life, in Keating's life. I just ignored that for a man who didn't love me. A man who treated Keating so terribly. Who treated my mother so terribly."

Shame inhales deeply. "Ahhhh. There's nothing like a spiral."

Shame's best friend Should shows up. They demand I make room on the couch, one on either side of me. Should looks nice enough. I wouldn't think she would be friends with someone like Shame, but I guess they're more alike than meets the eye. Should gets a whiff of my spiral and glances at Shame.

"You started without me." She sounds whiny, Should. Like a spoiled girl who didn't get her way. She tosses her perfect hair out of her perfect face. She looks like me. If I had done everything right. This is her power. She looks like how everyone tells me to look. She dresses how everyone tells me to dress. She speaks well. She sounds educated. Like she's gone to all those schools I dreamed of and gotten the degrees I'm so ashamed of not having.

Should smacks her gum and blows a bubble. She looks bored, but I know she's not.

"You should be grateful," she says casually. She loves to say her own name. "Some people don't have what you have. And even though you should've stood up for your brothers and your mom, you turned out okay. You should've gone to college, though. You should've used your brain for something. You're supposed to be smart."

She gestures to the open air in front of me. Shame's eyes are closed, his head resting on the back of the couch, a serene smile on his face.

"You should get a degree if you want people to take you seriously. You need credentials. You need clout."

"I don't care if people take me seriously. I just want them to know they're not alone. I felt really alone."

My shoulders slump. Shame stirs enough to pull some candy out of his pocket. They're melted, but I shove them in my mouth, embarrassed. Ashamed.

Shame studies her nails, not looking at me. She rarely looks directly at me. "You should really lose weight, Emerson."

I sigh around a mouthful of chocolate and caramel. "That's what you keep telling me."

Shame pokes my stomach. "What's that?"

Should snidely hands me a pillow. "You should cover that up. It's disgusting."

I start to say something about how Shame keeps giving me candy, but I forget – Should can read my mind.

"You don't have to eat it, you know. Besides, you should be in better shape, especially if you're not going to have kids. But you should have kids. You should be a mother."

I ball my fists up under the pillow.

"I don't want to have kids. I feel fulfilled without them."

Should glances at me out of the corner of her eye. "You shouldn't. That doesn't make any sense."

Shame chuckles to himself. "She loves to travel, Should. She has dogs. She has Taggart. She has her 'art.'"

He rouses himself enough to sarcastically put air quotes around 'art'.

Should joins in with a snide laugh. "Right! How could I forget?! She's a failed artist. And a terrible wife. Oh wait…." She cocks her head. "I think I'm stepping on your toes here, Shame."

He lazily blows a smoke ring. "You're good. We can share the duties. She's a lot of work, this one."

Should and Shame talk about me like I'm not there. They giggle. They whisper. I hear certain words.

Children.

Unlovable.

Stupid.

Uneducated.
Fat.
Lazy.
Insignificant.
Worthless.

They exhaust me so I lie down on the floor. They've taken over the couch now, sprawling, making themselves at home.

Depression curls up next to me on the ground, grabbing my hand, infusing me with their essence.

"You just need to take a nap,' Depression says. "You know Shame and Should. They could camp out here for days. Weeks."

I sigh plaintively. "They never clean up after themselves."

"I know." Depression holds my other hand.

"They always leave their stuff lying around."

I feel the emotion drain from me. I see Shame and Should so vividly. On my couch. Eating my food. Using my energy.

Depression pulls me into its embrace. "It's okay. I'm here."

Depression

Depression is the inability to construct a future. – Rollo May

I'm not sure if I'm entirely awake. It feels like I am but it also feels blurry in my mind, like an overcast day. There's a thick dense fog that I can almost see through, but not quite.

"You're up."

Depression comes in, sympathetic and understanding, carrying a mug of hot tea. I don't know if it's for me or for them, but the image is oddly comforting. Out of thin air almost they pluck a blanket, so welcoming in its texture that I instantly wrap it around myself when they hand it to me.

"Thank you," I murmur. I can't bring myself to speak above a whisper in here. "This is so nice of you."

Depression almost smiles, but not quite.

"You seem really familiar," I mumble.

My mouth feels foreign to me. Everything does.

"Have we met before? I feel like I've known you for years."

They bring the mug to their lips, then set it aside.

"It's too hot," They reply.

"That's how I like my beverages," I explain apologetically. "I'm a bit of an extremist sometimes."

Depression gives me a look of pity. They walk to the wall and dim the lights.

"I'm afraid that won't be the case for a while. We're just going to turn the volume down on life for a bit. It's too much right now."

"Oh. Okay."

I take this in stride. I'm so comfortable. Everything is soft and nothing is sharp. It feels palatable. Life has been so overwhelming for so long. So many colors. So many feelings. So many emotions. So many choices.

"You didn't answer my question."

Depression is rummaging through my clothes. "Hmmm? Oh, I suppose I didn't. Yes, Emerson. We've met before. I've known you for a long time, in fits and spurts. Especially that year you went to college. Remember when you would retreat to your dorm room and sleep for days at a time?"

I scratch my head. My hair is too heavy. Depression tosses me a hair tie. Without thinking, my hair goes up in a messy bun. I don't check to see how it looks. It doesn't matter.

"That was you? I thought I was just, you know. Tired."

They peek their head out of the closet with a shy grin. "Yes, that was me."

"Oh wow. Okay." At their gentle, encouraging gaze I snuggle deeper into the blankets.

Depression moving languidly, though with an alertness of a tending mother, comes to me.

"Why don't we get you another pillow, dear? Perhaps call it a day? We can talk more tomorrow."

My eyelids are heavy. I lay my head back and relax for the first time in what feels like years. Through my yawn I say, "Well, maybe just a nap. I am pretty tired."

Depression smiles to themselves. "Of course you are."

I open my eyes, but the room is dark. Not pitch black, but gray. Lots of gray. I see a note on my nightstand from my husband, Taggart.

It says "Get some rest. I love you."

It's next to a bottle of water, still cold from the fridge. I sigh and feel Shame start to come into view. I hear him whispering with Should. I recognize their voices. Just as they start to take shape, their voices rising to a normal pitch, Depression races in wiping their hands on an apron.

"Shoo! *Shoo*! You're far too extreme, Shame. You have to go. Should, you can stay of course, but just keep it low in the background, alright? We mustn't startle her."

"What's going on?"

My voice feels too loud. The texture of my jeans feels too rough. "How long have I been asleep? I need to get up."

Depression turns to see me. "You're awake. How delightful. What can I get you?"

Sitting on the side of my bed they come over, smelling lightly of fresh baked cookies and something else. Something I can't quite place. It smells off.

"Um, I'm kind of hungry. But I'll get it." I start to ease out of the bed, but Depression tucks me back in.

"I wouldn't hear of it. I'll fetch you something scrumptious. In the meantime, let's get you out of those clothes and into some pajamas, hmm?"

They hum lightly as my movements automatically coincide with what they suggest. My hands feel dense, like I've spent all day in a pool and just gotten out of the water to remember that I'm not actually weightless.

"Thanks. Let me just take a shower before I change." I begin to walk to the bathroom and try to find my shock when Depression redirects me.

They take my arm, gently, firmly, guiding me back to the bed.

"Let's just get these on you. Arms up, dear."

Lulled by their brisk matter of fact voice, my arms act of their own volition, and soon I'm wearing the most comfortable clothes I own. A t-shirt that is too big for me but feels like heaven, and cotton underwear. When I ask about pants, Depression tut-tuts me and just nudges me into bed.

Before I know it, I'm waking up again, the sun bright in my eyes. "What? What time is it?"

Depression waves the question away. "It doesn't matter. You need rest. You're so tired."

"I've slept so much though," I begin to protest, wincing at the harsh sounds of emotion. "I haven't even seen Taggart."

They chuckle softly. "Sure you did, dear. You spoke with him last night when he came in to kiss you goodnight. And again, this morning when he got up to make coffee. He's very sweet, your Taggart." Depression almost has a regretful twinkle in their eye.

"She should get out of bed. Maybe take a shower and pull herself together. Or have sex with her husband. Or oh, I don't know. Stop eating."

Should is in the corner, filing her nails, voice rising. She hates being ignored.

"Enough out of you. Emerson needs to rest, Should. Out."

Depression hustles Should from the room and turns around, sighing. "Finally. Now we can get some peace and quiet. Here, I've brought your laptop and keyed it up for your favorite show; the one you know all the lines to. And I've already told Taggart that you love him and you're sorry you're feeling so poorly. He just wants you to rest and take care of yourself. I've got everything covered. Don't worry about a thing. I'll take it from here."

Days go by like this. Eventually I get out of bed, but barely. I make it to the living room, but I don't put on pants. Depression says I don't need them because we don't have any plans today. When I think about all that Should told me to do, Depression turns down the color on the world, and things go from vivid, to the most nondescript shade of gray I've ever seen. I like gray. I tell Depression that and they laugh quietly, preening at my praise as if they've been waiting for this moment.

"How wonderful. Let's make everything gray then."

Before I know it, even I'm gray. I look in the mirror and see

Should. She's hiding from Depression, but she pops in occasionally. I think they work together. Should seems like she's got a lot of friends.

I wonder how *my* friends are. When was the last time I talked to them?

"Oh, yesterday. Don't feel badly if you don't remember, dear. I answered the phone for you."

Depression is bustling around the house, leaving trash and old dishes behind.

"You know," I say, really looking at them for the first time in a while. "You look like you've lost weight."

Depression glances sardonically from underneath their lashes. "Do I?"

"Yeah. And you look grayer. But a deeper, more tangible gray."

"Why, what a lovely thing to say." They walk over and kiss my cheek, their breath lingering. It smells sweetly fetid. Like rotted fruit and dirty dishes.

I lose track of time. I don't think to ask Depression how long they'll be around. They seem quite at home here, and really, I don't want to offend them. Just the thought of it makes me tired. Everything makes me tired. And hungry. And lethargic. I let it go. They're only around when it's just me, and it's just me a lot. I've made sure of that.

But one night, at dinner with Taggart, I look over at the next table and see Depression. They're all dressed up for the occasion, wearing my clothes. Taggart is trying to talk to me, but I can't stop looking at Depression. What are they doing here?

When I get home, I note that somehow, they're already there, ready to lay out my clothes, feed me dessert and tuck me in for the night.

For the first time, I don't want it. I tell Taggart about it, and he looks concerned. He asks how he can help. As he's asking the question, Depression grabs my hand. I can't seem to process what Taggart's asked. I know it's a question. I see on his face he's expecting an answer, but I don't have one. I shrug and tell him that I don't know. He hugs me, but Depression is still holding my hand. He tells me how much he loves me, but I don't feel it. I feel like that rhyme I heard in elementary school: *'I'm rubber and you're glue. Whatever you say bounces off me and sticks to you.'*

I hope he feels how much I love him. I can still feel that.

I lose track of time – *again*. I don't know how, but Depression does. They answer my phone now. They talk to my husband. They make him dinner. They even try to talk me out of my tradition of tucking love-notes in his suitcase when he travels for work. It takes almost everything I have, but I win that battle. Shame shows up again briefly when I realize that Depression is even in my sex life.

I don't cry. Not really. I'm irritable. I don't shower until I can smell myself or my fingers get stuck in my own knotted hair. I can't seem to feel much of anything. It's been a nice change, but lately I'm feeling confused. Taggart and I have been having problems. I've gained a lot of weight. Too much weight. He works even more, and I lose myself in shows that have too many seasons. Depression loves television.

Taggart and I are in couples counseling now. We almost get divorced — twice — but we don't. Our analyst, Dr. Q, talks to us both together and separately. I like it. I like him, even if Shame does come into the room to loom over me.

I don't want a divorce. I love my husband. My husband tells me that he doesn't know where I went. He tells me he doesn't know how to help me through this. He tells me he doesn't know how to love me through this. He tells me he doesn't know how to help me to *let* him love me. I feel this. I tell him I will try really hard. I know what I need to do. I just need to do it.

Depression didn't come to that session, though they tried.

Not long after, I'm talking with Dr. Q on my own. He asks me how I'm feeling. I tell him that I don't feel much. I feel like I should though. I tell him I know I'm not the same. I tell him I'm really confused, and I don't know what happened. I tell him that I know what I need to do, but I can't seem to do it. I tell him that I see what I need to do, and I want to do it so desperately, but it's on the other side of a brick wall. I tell him that I've tried everything I can think of to get to the other side of it — break it down, hunt up a ladder in an attempt to scale it, even painstakingly chisel a door — but the attempts only exhaust me.

I tell him that Shame shows up when I try. Shame shows up because even though I know I'm smart enough and capable enough to do those things, I can't. I feel like I'm one of those characters in a video game. I'm running against a wall with all my might even though I'm not going anywhere. But the wall doesn't move, and I don't know who is holding the controller to ask them to lift their finger and point me in the right direction.

Dr. Q uses the words 'Clinical Depression'. He tells me that Depression has been with me for a really long time, probably longer than even I realize. I don't tell him that I liked Depression at first. It felt familiar. Comfortable. When I think of that, Shame tries to come back in the room, even though he's not invited.

Dr. Q mentions medication and I balk. I go through the list point by point — what I'm worried about, what I'm afraid of. He patiently talks me through all my concerns and tells me that it's my decision. He tells me he only wants me to do what feels right to me and for me. He tells me that he cares about me.

I get irrationally angry when he tells me this. I have a tendency of getting really angry at Love, especially when I feel like I didn't do anything to earn it.

My eyes fill with hot tears, and before I can even think, I scream, "I fucking pay you to care about me!"

I've never screamed at Dr. Q before. I don't hear what he says after that. Depression came barreling into the room to smother me in their bosom the way they do when things go too sharp.

I don't tell Taggart about the outburst, and we do an emotional dance. A few steps forward, a few steps back. A few steps to the side that feel neither forward nor back, but they're steps, nonetheless.

Sometime later, I am triggered by a conversation I have with my older brother a few months before he dies. I fall apart, wailing incoherently on the couch. I don't have the energy to make it to a bathroom and cry in private like usual. Taggart sits next to me, holding me, telling me he loves me. I can't really feel that, but that's not unusual. Still, there is something that finally does reach me. What reaches me somehow, through the gray haze and blurred vision, is my husband's face. It is in perfect focus. But it's not just his face – that handsome face that I never tire of looking at. It's the expression on it. It's an expression he's worn for what seems like years, though it feels like I'm registering it for the first time.

He looks older. Drawn. Anguished — anguished that he can't pull me out of this hole that I'm in. He's in pain because he doesn't know how to help me. In that moment, I realize he can't help me, because I haven't helped me. I haven't been able to. And I don't just carry my pain, I'm cloaked in it. That cloak hides any semblance of who I once was. Who I truly am. Even from myself. Depression has muffled my pain with food, with blankets, with sleep that is never restful. I look at his face and realize the pain on his face is a pain I put there by not taking care of myself. In that moment, that split second moment that lasts an eternity, where I see my own torment which I am refusing to acknowledge etched on his beautiful face; I make a decision.

My next appointment with Dr. Q, I tell him I want to try medication. I don't remember telling him about that moment on the couch. I probably don't. But I know I have to do something to try to scale the wall. I have to do something to move myself forward.

He reassures me that the right medicine will not do what Depression does – numb me, make me unfeeling and irritable and lose my sex drive. That the right medicine will correct what's lacking in my brain chemistry so that I feel like myself. Dr. Q tells me that just because I take the medicine doesn't mean the work stops. Just the opposite. The medicine will show me a door in the wall so that I can walk through to what's on the other side.

I go home and I pack Depression's bags. There are a lot of them. I didn't realize how much they'd settled in. Depression makes a good case for themselves.

Do I really want to feel? What's so great about that?

Do I know what they're protecting me from?
It's safe with them.
They just want what's best for me.

I listen to their tirade dispassionately, and finally ask them, "Do you treat everyone like this?"

Depression stops mid-sentence, surprised by my question. "What do you mean?"

"Do you always start out so comforting and neutral, and then slowly take over everything until they feel alone and isolated?"

Depression looks offended. "No, of course not. Sometimes it's not slow. Or comforting. Or numbing."

"Ah. So, it's different for everyone."

"Yes, of course." Depression is patronizing now. "It's customized. Tailored to each person. Sometimes we stay a short while, sometimes we're there for years. And sometimes, we're rather intrusive and we're there from the beginning to the end."

They fold their clothes briskly, then turn almost apologetically.

"Emerson, I'm sorry to tell you, that I can't take everything."

I saw this coming. I know medicine and therapy aren't cures.

"I know," I say softly.

"I'm with you for quite a while I'm afraid, though my visits will become much less frequent. Not sure of the intensity yet. We'll have to play that by ear."

They come over to sit next to me on the bed where I've been watching them pack in a huff.

"I know that, too." I place my hand over theirs. It's sticky and its nails are bitten down to the quick. "It's just time for me to feel now. I need to feel everything. I can't do that with you here."

Depression walks out the door, leaving a trail of rumpled, fathomless puddles in their wake. I can see things, though. I can navigate around them. And if there are ones where I can't? That's okay. I know how to swim.

Grief

"What's that like? What's it taste like?
Describe it - like Hemingway."
"Well, it tastes like a pear. You don't
know what a pear tastes like?"
"I don't know what a pear tastes like to you."
— City of Angels

After Depression packed the majority of its bags, I waited. I waited for a long time. I'd be in a session with Dr. Q telling him how I wasn't sad. Or mad. I still didn't feel much of anything, which frankly that was a bit concerning to me.

This went on for quite a while, and while I didn't feel Depression's suffocating presence, I also didn't feel Loss around. She had been with me for so long, that it was almost like I stopped seeing her. Shame and Should were still loud as ever though; quietly insistent that I should be feeling something. Shame was more than willing to give Should a friendly reminder to prod me into action if I got too stagnant.

Suddenly, out of what seemed like nowhere, Loss knocks on my front door, holding a to go cup of coffee.

"Hi, Emerson. I know I've been gone for a bit, but I had an errand to run."

The blood drains out of my face.

"No. You're not coming in. You've done more than enough. I told you what would happen if you came back."

She waves her hand dismissively. "Oh, don't worry. I'm not here to stay. I have something I want to give you."

Confused, I glance at Loss, who is clearly waiting for something. She calmly sips her coffee, standing patiently on my porch.

"I know I make you uncomfortable. I'm sorry. I'm passing you off to someone else. They were supposed to be here a while ago, but they were delayed. That's when we called Depression. We asked them to extend their stay."

"I don't understand. Depression wasn't scheduled?" I rub my hands over my face trying to reconcile things. "They were here for such a long time. That was all just because this other person was late? I don't understand."

Loss paused. "I think I'll let your new ... friend speak for themselves."

"Friend? You're here to give me a friend? But...you're Loss. Why are you *giving* me anything?"

"It's complicated."

"Of course, it is," I declare sarcastically, throwing up my hands. "Why wouldn't it be?"

Shrugging, she cocks her head. "Ah, I hear him now."

Craning my head to look past her. I don't see anything.

"Where is he coming from?"

Loss's expression turns a bit sad now. "Everywhere."

"That doesn't make sense...." I began to laugh condescendingly when all the air is snatched from my lungs.

I find myself doubled over in the middle of gut-wrenching emotion. Something that feels like a combination of sadness, yearning, isolation, and despair.

Loss moves aside, careful not to touch me. "There you are. Finally!"

A hand clasps mine. "Pleased to meet you, Emerson. I'm Grief."

His hand is large, firm, and dry. He smells familiar. Comforting. I can't quite place it, but I feel like I've known him for years.

Loss looks from him to me, seemingly very content with what's just transpired.

"Alright," she said briskly. "I'm off then."

Left alone with my newfound Grief, I am swamped with all the feelings I hadn't felt when Depression was there. It almost makes me miss Depression, but part of me — the dark part of me that relishes these deep grooves of pain — wants this. It feels right. It feels…real.

Grief lets himself in, moving right past me to the dining room. He seats himself at the head of the table.

"What is this, some kind of a meeting?" I laugh to myself at how formal he is.

Grief's face is drawn with emotion. "Yes, Emerson. I'm afraid it is."

He sets a briefcase on the table, and opening it, pulls out a sheaf of papers. I can't read them, but I can tell they aren't empty.

"Before you ask any questions, please allow me to explain." Grief's voice is patient. "These contracts —"

"Contracts?" I interject.

"Yes, Emerson. Contracts. These are things that you signed." Lifting his hand to cease my sputtering objections, he continued. "I will explain. You loved your family, yes?"

Stunned by his question, I feel Shame's presence.

"Yes."

"Your mother Kate, your father Calvin, your brothers Charles and Keating." He slides sheets in front of me, one at a time to coincide with each family member. "These of course," gesturing to the other sheets on the table, "are for the whole. This one is for your family as a whole. This one is for your stepfather, Percy …"

"Wait. *Wait.* What does Percy have to do with anything?"

Protesting angrily, I try to push the sheet back in his direction. Somehow, the angrier I get and the more I try to move this particular piece of paper, the more writing appears on it.

Grief's face is pulled in sympathy. "You loved Percy, Emerson. You love him still." He pushes another sheet at me. "You love his family. They were your family for the foundational years of your life. For the majority of your life, in fact."

The wheels in my head turn as I process what he's telling me. He waits patiently - so patiently. It's as though he has all the time in the world. After what seems like forever, I finally put things together. Falling back in my chair, I stare at the ceiling, unwilling to look at the truth reflected back at me.

"I signed these contracts in Love."

Grief takes off his glasses. "Exactly."

"I understand. But I don't stop loving them because they're not here anymore. So does that mean that my Love for them is now tied to you?"

Grief doesn't say anything, just continues to look at me. I feel full of Love, remembering them individually, remembering things about them. But somehow, as I remember them, as I feel these things, the pit in my stomach becomes something like an emotional Grand Canyon. And there seems to be no end to this rough hollowness.

"No." I say clutching myself. "No. I can't. I can't feel this. I can't."

Grief reaches across the table to lay his hand on mine. "I'm so sorry for your Losses, Emerson. But I'm here for the duration."

I shake my head wildly, trying to make sense of it.

"The duration? What duration? The duration of the Loss? They're not going to stop being gone. So, what, you're here as long as they're gone? They're not coming back." My voice hitches and I start to choke on tears. "They're not coming back. So, you're here..."

Grief gets out of his chair, walks over to me and holds me in his arms.

"Yes. I'm here forever."

We stay like that for a long time. Me sitting in the chair, tears streaming down my face, the rough chasm of my heart somehow overflowing and emptying simultaneously. Grief is holding me, and it occurs to me that he's not going anywhere until I do. And even then, he will follow.

36

Taggart comes home from work, and I introduce them. Taggart is familiar with Grief. They briefly shake hands before I am flooded with the intimacy of Grief even though Taggart hasn't left the room.

Grief is more communicative than Depression. He's not numbing, but he is isolating. And consuming. I still live my life, but with the knowledge that I have a new shadow with me all the time.

In the beginning, Grief overtakes a lot of things. My mind, my heart, my Love. He uses it against me and reminds me of not only how much I love the loved ones that I have lost, but just how complicated everything really is. They're not coming back, and all the things that I see with Shame come up again. Grief and Shame don't get along. Grief is strangely protective of me, but I realize they work together like two coworkers in an office who have begrudgingly been thrown together on a project. Depression comes back a bit more often, but they're afraid of the emotions that Grief brings.

Everything is so vivid, so clear, so painstakingly unavoidable.

When the Christmas season comes around again and Taggart has to go on an essential business trip for a few days, I'm home alone. I love when he goes out of town. I pretend I live alone again, blaring music at 3:00 a.m. when I can't sleep, and watching the same movies over and over. Depression taught me that trick and it's something that's stuck with me.

This is the first Christmas season that's come since Grief showed up and I forget about him for a while. I treat myself to a fancy hot chocolate and start shopping for Christmas presents in earnest.

I cannot emphasize how much I love doing this. Usually there is a gray fog when I do, and I've tried - somewhat successfully - to push through it in the past. This year it's different. I feel like me. Giving myself over to the process of selecting the perfect gifts, the perfect wrapping paper and the coordinating ribbons, I think I'm in the clear. That's when Grief shows up.

"Wouldn't that be perfect for your mom?" He points to a particularly Kate looking item. It's a pendant for a necklace - tiger's eye, round, smooth. I can see her wearing it with her favorite green wool sweater, hands reaching up to worry it absently as she talked or read.

I stare at it, the pit in my stomach rising to my chest.

"Wow, that really does look like her." Without thinking I reach for it.

"You can't give it to her." Grief places his hand over mine — the one that's still in midair reaching. With his hand on mine, I am both pulled toward the necklace and further away from it. I won't see it on the background of that favorite sweater, her perfume tickling my nose as she hugs me to thank me for it. Still, the stone finds its way into my hand. Maybe if I just walk around with it. I don't have to buy it. I can just pretend ...

"She's not here, Emerson."

"Right. Right." I shake my head like a baffled dog.

I do another loop through the store, and I realize Grief has begun to shift. He's no longer the proper fellow with the briefcase handing me contracts. He's a child, running through the store pointing out things.

"Oh, this would be perfect for Charles! Could you just imagine him in this?"

He's pointing to a particularly flashy ensemble, bright with color, begging to be noticed. A watery laugh comes out, unbidden.

"Only Charles could pull that off. He really loves those bright colors and patterns."

Reaching out to touch the fabric, I close my eyes. Loved, I correct myself. Still, I find myself trying to imagine what Charles would look like today. I can't. Before I can shake it off, Grief is onto the next thing.

"Oh, what about this for Keating? He was always so meticulous with those fancy tastes of his."

It's a watch, extravagant in its austerity.

I sigh to myself. "It really does look like Keating, but I'm not spending that kind of money on one person."

I lift my phone to snap a picture to send to Keating. He loves these sorts of things - the kinds of things that tell the world how successful he has become. I can hear his response upon receiving the picture - that signature Keating cackle of glee. I pull up his contact information in my phone, and as I begin to type out a message Grief snatches the phone from my hand.

"What the hell?" I'm pissed. "What do you think you're doing?"

Grief, still holding my phone, deletes Keating's contact. A scream is ripped from my throat as I attack him.

"What the fuck are you doing?!"

He hands my phone back to me, pulling me against him.

"You can't send that to him."

I continue to fight Grief right there in the store as he swaddles me like an emotional straitjacket, waiting for me to wear myself out. I finally do. Exhausted, immobilized, it hits me. Not only do I not get to buy Keating the watch, but I don't get to send him the picture, either. Grief is doubling down.

Tears spring to my eyes and I look at the things in my arms. Lost in the avalanche of emotion, I forgot to remember that I don't have a reason to purchase these. Grief brings me further into his embrace, guiding me around the store as I put the things back on the shelves. He spends the rest of the day with me, even though I had planned for it to be fun and festive.

I go through the motions, grateful to Depression for teaching me how to run on autopilot. I go home and turn on my favorite Christmas movie. I make another hot chocolate with all the trimmings. I put on incredibly cozy clothes. I start to lay out the presents I did get around to purchasing and the Christmas accoutrements that go with them. I keep seeing the ones I didn't get to buy, but I remind myself that I love this.

You love wrapping presents; I tell myself over and over again as I try to reclaim the joy. I diligently select paper for each person, a coordinating ribbon, a cute name tag, signing both my and Taggart's names. This is one of my favorite things about Christmas. But this year, oh this year, Grief is here. He's sprawled on my couch, eating popcorn, watching me watch the movie.

"This is supposed to be fun," I tell him. "Would you mind leaving me to my day?"

He points to the pile of presents. "There aren't any presents for your family. That's all for Taggart's family."

"They are my family." Protesting vehemently, I re-tie the bow that his statement caused me to fumble.

Grief snorts and shovels more popcorn into his mouth.

"Yeah, for what? A couple of years? Do they know how Percy's mother made lasagna on Christmas Eve? Do they remember how you made coffee and blueberry muffins for Kate and Percy at 5:00am every Christmas morning? Or how you and Keating stayed up all night dancing around? Or how you tucked Charles in when he fell asleep on your bed? Or how you and Keating and Charles made sled ornaments out of popsicle sticks and toothpicks with Kate? Or how Charles –"

I cut him off. "Stop saying his name."

I briefly wish for the numbness of Depression as I sink into memories. Painting popsicle sticks and gluing them together with Mom while Bing Crosby longs for snow. Percy yelling at Keating for sleeping away Christmas afternoon because we were up all night laughing and dancing in our bedrooms. The smell of Mom's coffee as she watched us open the gifts, she'd carefully selected for us. Charles' smile through the years as he opens toys, then clothes, and eventually fuzzy dice to hang from the mirror of his first car. Keating's delighted cackle at a talking Buzz Lightyear figurine. '*To infinity - and beyond!*' Mom's teary eyes at a gardening book. Percy's gleeful joy at a whoopee cushion and t-shirts with hilarious sayings. Eating the muffins that have gone cold in the excitement of red and green paper. I get lost in twenty-five years of Christmases until …

"But…you're not wrapping any presents for your own family."

Taking in the clutter all around me, I think of the items I put back. I think of how Taggart's family doesn't know that Santa prefers peanut butter cookies. Or how we always got peppermint patties in our stockings. Or how we spent the rest of the day watching A Christmas Story over and over. The clawing in my stomach returns.

"I don't have any family to buy presents for." I say this quietly, almost to myself.

I make the habitual objections in my head to this statement; *I have friends who I consider family. Taggart's family is my family.* But Grief knows me so well. He knows exactly what I'm thinking.

"Emerson, they have their own families. They love you. They really do. But they've all got their own holiday family traditions. Even if you were invited, you'd just be what you are when you're with Taggart's family - a voyeur, longing to belong. And you almost do. Almost." Grief abandons his popcorn, coming over to wrap me in his familiar hug.

"Why are you so comforting and so painful all at the same time?"

And there, alone on the floor surrounded by slivers of wrapping paper and discarded bows, the tinny music of my favorite childhood Christmas movie playing in the background, I succumb.

"If you weren't married, Emerson what would you do for Christmas?"

"But I am married. I am loved. I have a wonderful husband. I have my own family…"

Should shows up then, plucking up a piece of popcorn.

"You think one person is a family? A husband? He should be here with you."

Annoyed, I tell her that she's unwelcome here.

"I like when Taggart goes out of town."

She looks at the pile of presents disdainfully. "He shouldn't have left you alone on Christmas."

"It's not Christmas," I remind her. "And this is the life we both chose. This is how we designed it, together. It's not like he created this life and I just tag along. We make these choices together. Besides, I like being alone. It's fun."

Should looks over at Grief. Grief holds me tightly, almost suffocatingly. "It's good you like being alone. Because you are."

From then on doesn't matter whether Taggart is out of town or not. Grief always spends the holidays with us.

Each time we go back to Ohio to visit Taggart's family, I see the exit we would take to visit Percy. Grief grabs my hand each time, and I suppress the urge to cry. Out there somewhere, Percy and the family I used to spend so much time with are still living, still laughing, still spending time together. The only thing that's missing is me.

"Am I really missing if they don't miss me? If they made the decision to call Loss together, how do I still love them?"

Shame shows up then, flexing his fingers. He's always ready to get into it. I talk with him and Grief, because I'm confused. I understand that Grief is around a lot because of Mom, Charles, and Keating.

"I understand that I miss them. I miss what could be. I understand that I love them. I understand that because I love them so deeply still, Grief, you are more tangible when I think of them. Or even when I'm not thinking of them, and you pop in out of nowhere. I'm beginning to understand that I can't possibly prepare for you, Grief. I never know how long you'll stay; I never know what form you'll take or how you'll make me feel."

Grief nods. "Good. It's good you understand that, because since they're never coming back, I'm never leaving."

My stomach clutches. "Can you stop saying 'they're never coming back'? That might help."

Grief sighs. "I can't do that."

"Fine," I remark, pushing that down to deal with later. "What I don't understand is what you're doing here when I think of Percy?"

Grief looks to Shame. Shame is silent. Watching. Judging. Looking for weakness.

Grief sits with me. "Emerson, you remember the contract?"

"Yes."

"You signed it in Love."

"I know."

He looks at me. Then he looks at Shame.

"Shame is here because you still love Percy. You still love Percy's family. They were yours for twenty years, and in many ways, they still are. You were just five when you met them. And then when you needed them most, they called Loss and asked her to take you from them. They made that decision together. Without you. They didn't want you anymore."

I don't say anything, and Shame plays the movies again.

"But...Percy was so cruel to Keating. And even my mom. And with me..."

My voice trails off. No one speaks for a while and Grief pulls me into his clinging hold.

"They were the family you grew up with. He was the father you were allowed to love. And you loved him so much, Emerson. You loved your grandmother. Your grandfather. Your aunts and uncles. You loved them so much."

For the first time, I look to Shame to save me. I don't want to feel these things. Shame blows his smoke rings and has the audacity to wink at me.

"But ..." I start to protest, pointing to the screen of memories in my head that only Grief and Shame and I can see.

"That doesn't negate how much you love them. They were your family, for better or worse. And you don't stop loving them because they leave you. But my role in your life with Percy is very different. It's a bit more complex because you're mourning him even though he's still alive, still out there living his life. He's moved on. He's gotten remarried. He has a new stepdaughter. He's happy. And you're...not."

I cling to Grief, confused in this solace. He understands me in a way I don't. I hear Should show up again, but my face is buried in Grief's shoulder, thinking of all the Love I'm missing out on from Percy. Wondering if I ever received any at all.

"You should be happy though, Emerson. Look at your life."

She shows me my gorgeous, understanding, kind, supportive husband. She shows me the traveling that we do. She shows me the freedom I have, the things I don't have to worry about. She starts to berate me, telling me I should be grateful that I have what I have. She tells me that there are so many other people who have it so much worse than I do.

Grief starts to fight with her and holds me even tighter when Should and Shame try to pry me from his arms.

This is how things go for a long time. I live in this limbo for years.

Grief shows up when I'm in Paris. Mom always wanted to come to Paris. Keating and I talked about taking her before she died, but I didn't have the money and Death came too quickly for us to be able to. Shame shows up, so loud, so clear, since I'm so sad in this place that I've dreamed of seeing for years. One day in Paris I fight with Taggart. He leaves to explore, and I lay in bed all day with Should and Depression.

Grief shows up when a Whitney Houston song comes on the radio and catapults me back to a moment where Keating would dance around ridiculously. When I see someone struggle with addiction or suicidal thoughts, Grief is always there, reminding me of Keating. When I see tow-headed children shrieking with glee, holding hands, or whispering in each other's confidence, I'm reminded of how close Keating and I once were. Unfortunately, Shame is right behind him, reminding me that I didn't help Keating. Shame often asks if I have the right to spend so much time with Grief when I still love Percy given how he treated my brother. Given how I didn't do anything to stop it.

Grief and Shame show up when I think of Percy. It's not often, but when I think of my foundational family, I miss them. I talk to Grief about how we would spend holidays at his mother's house. He shows me how I called her 'Grandma' for twenty years. Grief reminds me of the tire swing at her house, and I tell him how I used to go to her house early on Thanksgiving to help. I tell Grief how Percy used to make me laugh, and Grief reminds me of music Percy introduced me to. When I smell motor oil or hear a motorcycle, Grief's nostalgia is especially present.

Shame gets annoyed when Grief starts without him. This invariably brings up Shame about how my relationship with Grief is stronger for Percy than for Calvin. Should tells me all the things I should have done, and that if I had done any number of them, then perhaps I would mourn a great father. A father who wanted me, who fought to stay for me, who loved me; instead of one who left me of his own accord. Grief is confusing around Calvin.

Grief shows up more often for Charles than anyone except my mother. He's always around, whispering Charles' name, reminding me that Charles isn't here. That Charles will never grow up. Or visit my home. That Charles will never have a family of his own. There are certain songs and movies and smells that bring Grief in. Sometimes for just a moment, sometimes for hours. Grief reminds me how Charles was so kind, so bright, so young.

And just as Grief hits his stride and consumes me to a shattering degree, Should shows up and tells me it was my job to take care of my little brother. Shame reminds me that I didn't. Should and Grief spend a lot of time with me when I think of Charles. Should tells me that if I had just done this, if I had just been there, Charles would still be here, too. Grief is particularly sharp around Charles. He's not comforting. He's persistent, nagging, poking me even when I relax. Sometimes I even think I see Charles out of the corner of my eye. Grief doesn't let me say Charles' name for a few years. I cry when I try, and it comes out broken. Like me.

Grief is purer for my mom; less Shame, less Should, but the depth and vivacity of Grief is overwhelming. Grief smells like her a lot: her favorite perfume, cigarette smoke, coffee. I see Grief when I look down at my hands. Her hands. I feel Grief when I rearrange pillows or furniture, remembering all the times we did that growing up. Grief stands behind me in the mirror when I brush my teeth, making me realize how much my face looks like hers. Grief holds me particularly tightly in Autumn when everything smells like her somehow; earthy and deep. Grief grips me when I bake Christmas cookies or make my favorite birthday meal. Grief shows up when I read a book that we talked about, or even ones we didn't but I know she'd love. Grief makes me buy the books she read to me as a child, and I hear her when I read the words. I know she wasn't perfect, but Grief still causes me to yearn for my mother no matter how old I get.

Grief was right when he told me he'd be with me forever. As

time goes on, there are days where it feels like he might be gone. There are situations that would previously have brought Grief around instantaneously, where he shows up a little less strongly, and the visit may not be as long. But then, inexplicably, something I thought would be safe, something unrelated, brings him in and he is so clear that I try to fight him. I yell at him, I throw things at him, but he won't go unless he's ready.

Sometimes I even invite Grief in to sit with me.

"I know it sounds so strange for me to ask you to come here," I tell him, handing him a drink.

"Nothing is strange to me," He reassures me.

"You're the only one who knows them as well as I do."

I select a movie that makes him particularly poignant. We sit together for a long time. I point out certain scenes, bringing up memories that only he and I know about.

Grief is as real to me as the ground beneath my feet. He is the only connection I have to these loved ones that I've lost and the family I lost with them. So sometimes I invite him in and embrace the waves that come with him; the sadness, the affection, the abandonments, the complexities, the longing, the yearning; the intangible things that are so real to me they are tattooed onto both skin and soul. Grief's presence reminds me that once, however long ago, my mother, my father, Charles, Keating, even Percy, were once real people in my life. That I didn't dream them up. And now that all I have left of them are memories, he's the only one left to share them with. So as painful as Grief is – and he is – he's better than pretending that they were never here.

Fear

*You've gone a million miles; how far would you get - to that
place where you can't remember, and you can't forget?*
– Bruce Springsteen, Secret Garden

*W*hat if I forget them?

This is the recurring thought that lives in my head.
It's already happening, little by little. I remember some
things so clearly; the name of my mother's signature perfume, the
bright gold that hugged Charles' pupil before bursting into a gorgeous
blue, the way Keating scrubbed at his head when he was excited; but
other things are fading. I can no longer remember the exact timbre
of my mother's voice when she said my name. Or which Metallica
song was Charles' favorite. Or the last time Keating and I had a
conversation that didn't end in a fight.

Shame shows up on the days when I am so deeply entrenched
with Grief that I beg him to leave. For every time I invite Grief to sit
and reminisce, there are three times that I have tried everything to
kick him out. I have told Grief that I'm glad my family is gone. I tell
Grief that they hurt me so deeply, that they fucked me up so much,
that my life is more peaceful now. I yell at Grief on these days, telling
him all the new things Shame has locked and loaded. He's been

hoarding the other side of Grief's memories – the bad ones I bury deep down inside. The ones where I'm glad I don't get manipulated into giving Mom money. The ones where I feel like I can breathe without worrying about Charles now that he's somewhere safely out of my responsibility. The ones where I am so relieved that I don't have to worry about getting those phone calls in the middle of the night anymore. I already got them.

More often than not the bitter words I yell at Grief come out while I'm scraping the bottom of a pint of ice cream. I can tell Shame loves it. When this happens, he gets so high on these thoughts that he can't move for months.

I want to forget them. And I want to remember every single detail. And at any given moment, I feel every variation of both of these.

Loss has come and taken things in the name of Grief; my waistline, my independence, my ability to be present. I'm still here, deep down. She hasn't taken me completely. I fight her every single day. But I'm exhausted. I'm losing myself in Grief. It's defining my life. And with every single thing that I give to Loss in the name of Grief, something is put in its place. Something I have known all my life.

Fear.

Fear is cold and lonely. They're loud and quiet at the same time, and I don't know how they do it. I've never met something that makes no sense and so much sense simultaneously.

Fear sounds so much like me, even more than Should. Fear sounds so much like me – all the versions of me that I have ever been – that I have trouble discerning which voice is mine and which voice belongs to them.

Fear loves giving me questions and filling out the answer before I even have the time to think. They've got an answer for everything. Fear is a know-it-all. And boy, do they think they know it *all*.

Fear doesn't show up the way the others do. It shows up like Loss: when I least expect it. It shows up with Should, posing questions to myself, offering comparisons that I didn't ask for. It shows up with Shame, making me afraid not only of myself, but the ones I love. It shows up like Depression: under the guise of helping me cope, helping me protect myself. It shows up like Grief: sharply poignant. Softly insistent.

Fear is something I know very well. They have permeated every aspect of my life, whether I want them to or not. And it has never occurred to me that I could be allowed to not want them there because, like any good fungus, Fear evolves and learns me. It knows what I need to hear to keep them around. I can't understand Fear, but Fear understands me. Fear has made a study of me since before I was even born, using facts, logic, and history to its advantage. Fear has receipts. Fear has proof. Fear doesn't just show up. Fear always there, humming constantly in the background until it turns the volume up on itself.

I've long since stopped noticing Fear. Or more accurately, I've long since stopped noticing that I noticed Fear. Fear has become a part of me, imprinted into the very fabric of who I am. Fear did this the way people fall in love – inevitably and without warning.

"That's so romantic Emerson," Fear croons to me. How quickly I forget that they know the inner workings of my mind so well. After all, they were involved in the construction.

"I really enjoy our time together," Fear continues.

I feel a shivery stroke down my spine. Goosebumps break out on my skin.

"I'm just trying to protect you."

"From what?" I can't help but ask. I never get the answer I want to this question, but somehow, they make me feel like they've answered it. Fear talks like a politician - giving answers without actually answering the question at hand.

"Pain, darling. If we prepare for it, then we're ready."

"We were prepared for Mom to die, but it still hurt." The words spill from my mouth before I realize what I've said.

We.

Fear's smile is sharp and indulgent.

"Yes, we were. But we weren't prepared for Charles. Or Percy and his family abandoning us. Or Keating. Or Calvin. Now I know what you're going to say – they died. But what if *Taggart* dies? What will we do then? How will we cope? Then you'll really be alone!"

My eyes are wide with shock.

"How can you even think of that?! I don't even want to entertain the thought."

I try to run away from Fear, but they are dogged.

"I'm just trying to make sure we aren't blindsided again. He drives so much. Do you know how common car crashes are? How often people are killed in those car crashes?"

Fear puts an image in my mind.

A ten-car pileup. Taggart is at the bottom, immobile and unresponsive. Then it's a slick, ice-covered road where Taggart skids and dies in slow motion. Next, it's Taggart walking in the door, healthy and happy. He's leaving. For good. Taggart tells me I'm not enough and I am too much at the same time. I'm too much work for not enough reward. I'm too depressed and not happy enough. I've lost too much of myself to Grief. The girl he fell in love with was whole, unbroken. I'm too big, not small enough. I'm too awkward, not graceful enough. I'm too crass, not educated enough.

In all of these images, I am alone and rejected. Left by the person I love the most. I won't need to run to the bathroom and lock the door, hiding my muffled cries in a towel anymore. I'm in the living room, but there is no life to be living. It's just the sound of the guttural howls ripping from deep within me because – just as Fear told me they would – Loss and Death have come to take another person I love. A person who claims to love me purely, without reason.

Fear has an endless supply of images like this. And as I picture them, as I irrationally believe them, I remember when Fear first came to me.

I was little, too little to really know what was going on. We hadn't seen Calvin in a couple years, and after a few days of court ordered visitation with him, Keating and I had fallen back into old patterns. Calvin had taken us swimming in his hotel pool and launched us into the air with his banter of flight checks.

"Spruce Goose, lookout! Here comes Keating, growing like a weed!"

Keating's classic high-pitched squawk - something I hadn't heard in so long - was drowned out as he landed into the water with a massive splash.

Calvin chased me around the pool with the promise of an even bigger launch. I jump in to escape him, and he's right behind me.

"Watch out, Princess! It's the monster!"

He grabbed my foot under the water and pulled me to him. The smell of his cologne and his whiskered chin tickled my senses, and before I knew it, I squealed, "Dad! Stop!"

He did stop - just long enough to pull me into a tight hug before launching me into the air.

After that, it felt weird to call him Calvin. He was Dad. He was the smell I remembered when I thought of my dad. He was the dad who had read to me and lifted me on his shoulders so could run after Keating and Mom, sending them into fits of giggles. He was the one who had made me soup when I was sick and chased Mom around the kitchen with shaving cream on his face, begging for a kiss.

Keating had flatly refused to call him Calvin, but I had been torn. With one familiar, sensory moment, I had followed my own instincts and done what had felt natural.

It was a beautiful day, replete with the joy and love of family intimacy. One I remember with such clarity it's as though it just happened. When we got home Mom and Percy sat us down in the living room and asked us about our visit. Keating didn't say much, but I was overjoyed and couldn't wait to share.

"We had the best time! We went swimming and got to pretend we were airplanes and cannonballs. I was a mermaid. Dad even swam with me on his shoulders! I was so tall!"

I looked at Mom and Percy, waiting for them to be happy that we had such a nice time, but they said nothing. They leaned against the breakfast bar, the silence stretching until I developed a feeling in the pit of my stomach. They were upset, I could tell. I didn't know why, but this feeling in my stomach didn't feel good to my nine-year-old body.

After a while, Mom spoke.

"When did you start calling him Dad?"

Keating poked me and I could see his eyes widen in a way that mirrored the feeling in the pit of my stomach. I didn't know it yet, but it was Fear.

"Um, I don't know." I looked down and started tracing patterns in the carpet with my fingers.

"Percy is your dad. You really hurt Percy's feelings, Emerson."

Before I could think, Keating cried out, "Why can't we have two? Some kids at school have two Dads. How come we have to choose?"

Staring defiantly at Mom and Percy, Keating didn't back down.

"Percy isn't our dad. Calvin is. Dad is our dad. Percy is our stepdad."

Percy said nothing, but his gaze was on Keating. Mom gasped and whispered, "Where did you hear that?"

"Dad told me," Keating admitted. "He said he would always be our dad because we're part of him. Even if we don't talk to him or see him, he's always going to be our dad. Even if we're old and he's not around, he's always going to be our dad."

I reached over to hold Keating's hand and found it slick with sweat.

"That's not true," Mom said. "A Dad is someone who loves you even if they don't have to. Percy doesn't have to love you. But he does. Percy doesn't have to be here and take care of us, but he does. Calvin doesn't want to see you ..."

"You're lying!" Keating's face was wet with tears. He let go of my hand as he got to his feet. Looking up at him from the floor, I saw that hand ball into a fist. "He said he wants to see us. He said he calls all the time, but you tell him we don't want to talk to him. He said you tell him we don't want to see him. He said you tell him that we're mad at him. I'm not mad at him. I'm mad at you!"

Mom starts crying and Percy wraps his arms around her.

"Keating, look what you did. You made your mom cry. How could you hurt her feelings like this? You don't get to talk to her like that."

He reaches behind Mom's trembling shoulders and grabs a wooden spoon. Mom doesn't look at us and takes it from Percy.

"Keating, you're not allowed to talk to me like that."

She pulls him over to the couch, slides down his pants, and lays him across her lap. She hits him on the butt with the wooden spoon over and over. He's crying. She's crying. I'm crying and begging her to stop.

After Keating's butt is bright red, she sends him to his room and tells him he's grounded.

I get up to follow but Percy tells me to stay.

Mom is crying so hard her entire body is shaking. Percy crouches to my level. He tells me that Keating hurt his feelings. That Keating hurt Mom's feelings. He tells me that he just wants to be a good Dad to us. That he just wants Mom to be happy. Don't I want Mom to be happy?

I nod when he says this. I do want her to be happy. I like it when she's happy. Her laugh is deep and rich and makes me think of October.

Percy hugs me. "Don't you want us all to be happy, Emerson?"

I want to say that Keating isn't happy. I want to say that Calvin isn't happy. I want to say that I'm confused, but I know that I'll get in trouble if I do. I don't want to get in trouble. I don't want to get hit with the spoon. Besides, I love Mom. I love Percy for making my mom happy and for making her laugh. He didn't make her cry. Keating did. Right?

I nod. I do want everyone to be happy. Maybe if Mom is happy then Keating will be happy.

"Good girl," Percy says. "I love you, Emerson. I'm glad you're my daughter."

It's the first time he's said he loves me. It's the first time he's called me his daughter. It feels good. He doesn't have to love us, Mom had said. Isn't it better that he doesn't have to and he does?

"I love you too, Dad."

From then on, Percy is Dad. Keating slips up sometimes and one time Percy took the spoon from Mom because she was crying too hard to hit Keating. That's when the spoon broke over Keating's butt, he peed his pants and Percy called him a name I'd never heard before.

"See?" Fear brings me back to the present. "If you hadn't listened to me, you would've ended up like Keating. Instead, you and Percy had a great relationship."

"But we didn't. He's not around anymore. He doesn't have to love me anymore, so he doesn't."

Fear is quiet for a moment while they think. "Well, what did you do?"

"Excuse me?"

"You must've done something to make him stop loving you. What if you actually said all those awful things about his family? The ones he told you that you said?"

I shake my head. "I think I'd remember saying cruel things about my own family - especially when they were the only family I had left."

Fear puts images I've never seen in my head. While I don't believe the images, Fear knows me well enough to know where to strike.

"What about those things you say to Taggart when you're mad?"

"We're human, Fear. We fight. No one is perfect. We're just … figuring each other out. Marriage is hard."

"Well, he only proposed to you because he felt bad for you."

I yank at the roots of my hair. "That makes no sense. Why would someone commit to me for the rest of their life out of pity? Taggart isn't like that."

Fear crouches in front of me again and looks me directly in the eye.

"You thought Percy wasn't like that. You still call him 'Dad' in your head."

"That's different." But I'm not so sure.

"He didn't have to love you. Neither does Taggart. How many times have you almost gotten divorced now?"

"Only twice. And almost doesn't count," I say, defending my marriage. "He loves me."

"He loves the girl who had a life of her own. He loves the thinner girl who worked all the time and had friends. Now that you've moved in with him, he's your whole world. This isn't what he signed up for. Look at you."

Fear shows me what I look like. Shame shows up then, Should not far behind.

"Do you want Loss to take your marriage?" Fear asks me gently. I hate when Fear is gentle.

"No. She won't. I won't let her."

Shame and Should laugh. "Like you have control over that," Shame retorts. "You don't even have enough control to make sure you shower and get dressed every day."

I'm swallowed up by Fear. The longer they're there, the clingier I get to Taggart. It only makes things worse.

I tell Dr. Q about Fear, because I have to tell someone. I've told Taggart about Fear, and my beautiful defender of a husband does his best to get rid of them. He can't and eventually he feels like he can't do anything right. I've made him feel that way because Grief has energized Fear to the point that Fear has morphed into something else entirely. A hybrid. Dr. Q calls this Anxiety.

Soon, Anxiety has me in its clutches and I don't know what's real. I don't trust myself. I don't trust that I'm good enough for Taggart. If I wasn't good enough for my dad to stay - either Dad - then how can I be good enough for this kind person who is so intelligent and so motivated?

Anxiety tells me I'm better off leaving Taggart. He makes me bite my nails until they bleed and tells me that Taggart deserves someone thin and beautiful and intelligent. That Taggart is stuck with this version of me and that it's not fair to him. Anxiety has me mourning the loss of a marriage that I'm still in and I'm so confused.

My anti-depressants and Dr. Q help with this, and within a few months Anxiety becomes Fear again. Fear, I know. Fear, I'm comfortable with. I tell Dr. Q that Fear is just the other side of Love, and Dr. Q cocks his head at me. He asks me to expand but I don't know how. I don't know why I believe that, but I do.

"Take me through this, Emerson." Dr. Q is very interested in this concept.

"How do you mean?" I don't know what exactly he's asking for. How can I take him through something that is so ingrained in me? Something I don't even have logic for?

I try to make a joke and brush it off. I make a lot of jokes about Fear and Love, and well. Everything. Dr. Q doesn't laugh, but one day he might.

"Why do you think that Fear is just the other side of Love?" He puts his pen down and folds his hands together. I have his undivided attention. It makes me even more uncomfortable. He knows this and is betting on my discomfort to fill the silence between us. It's an emotionally vulnerable standoff, and whoever talks first wins. Fear doesn't want me to win.

"Don't talk first." Fear whispers in my head. "He doesn't understand us. I'm just trying to protect you."

I visibly shake my head to try to unseat Fear.

"Fear is just protecting me. Fear makes sure I don't do anything to lose someone's Love or hurt someone's feelings."

Dr. Q's gaze is steady on mine. The air between us is thick with something important, but I'm not sure I'm ready for it.

"You think that you can do something to cause someone to stop loving you?"

It's such an obvious answer that I laugh. "Well, yeah."

I tell him about my first memory of Fear. Fear is trying to stop me from sharing something so personal, so intimate, but I'm on my pedestal.

Dr. Q is really quiet. He looks at me with sympathy, but I see pity. This is when he uses words like 'emotional abuse' and 'gaslighting' and 'conditional love.'

He asks me if anyone could do anything to make me stop loving them and I say no. He asks me to sit with that, to think why the reverse could be true for me. I try to answer his question, but Grief comes in followed by Shame. How could I be thinking such terrible things about people who aren't alive anymore? They're dead. Isn't that enough?

I let Grief take over the session then. Fear smugly stands next to me, a hand on my shoulder. "Good girl."

I go home and think more about it. I've never loved someone and not been scared they would leave. I loved my grandparents, and they died. I loved Calvin and he died. I loved Mom and she died. I loved Keating and he died. I loved Charles and he died. I loved Percy and his family and though they were still alive, they left. Fear had logic on their side. It was just a matter of time until my friends and my husband died or left, and I was truly alone. So, wasn't it just better to be alone in my mind and prepare for it?

"I don't want to do that," I tell Fear.

"What are you going to do, Emerson? Tell everyone how I make you feel? Do you know how pathetic and insecure that makes you sound? You can't tell anyone about our conversations. They'll just think you're needy and overly sensitive."

Fear shows me times I would get upset when Mom would read my journal. When Percy told me I couldn't be a writer because it wasn't a real job. When Keating got older and would yell at me when no one was around, grabbing me so hard I would get bruises.

"You're too sensitive. It's in my house so it's my property. I can read it if I want to." Mom would say.

"You're too sensitive. I'm just trying to help you manage your expectations." Percy would say.

"You're too sensitive. I'm just playing around." Keating would say.

I learned to stop keeping a journal and write fiction. Mom would still read it and question me, asking me if this is how I really felt. Fear would make me lie to her and tell her that it was fiction. It wasn't real. I read a lot of books. I just had a good imagination. Fear told me if I told her the truth, she wouldn't love me either. She would send me away to live with Calvin – someone I had heard dozens of terrible stories about – stories laced with drugs, alcohol, and abuse. By the time I turned fourteen I was terrified of him.

I learned to write for fun and stop talking about what I wanted to be when I was older. I listened to Mom and Percy when they told me what I should be when I grew up. I listened to them when they told me what to major in in college. I listened to them when I came home from college and they told me it was because I wasn't good at it, not because they didn't fill out the financial aid paperwork. Fear told me not to fight with them about it, because they'd leave like Calvin did. But I didn't keep it shut that time. And that's how I ended up living with a boy who liked to hurt me, answering clandestine phone calls from Charles in the middle of the night because he wasn't allowed to talk to me.

So I learned to keep my mouth shut. About a lot of things. I didn't speak up for Keating when Percy hurt him. Or when Percy's friends laughed at him and called him names. I didn't tell anyone about Keating hurting me or making me cry. He would only get in more trouble, and I didn't want to be responsible for more of his pain.

"I taught you how to take care of yourself," Fear often told me. "If it wasn't for me, how would you have gotten this far?"

I didn't answer. I didn't know if there was one.

"You've been with me for as long as I can remember," I told them. "In the way I saw Keating being treated. In the loving way I saw Charles being treated. You made me think that if I did everything they asked me to do, and more, that they would love me the way they loved Charles. And if I didn't, they would treat me like they treated Keating."

"You take care of the people you love, Emerson. You have to take care of them first. They come first. Your feelings and needs come last. Otherwise, they won't love you anymore. They stopped loving Keating because he wasn't what they wanted. Be what everyone else wants. If you do that, they'll love you."

"How can I be that to everyone? How can I make everyone happy at the same time if they have different needs?"

Fear shrugged. "It's not my job to figure that out. It's yours."

I sit with this thought for a long time. In the quiet din of my mind when Shame and Should are occupied, when Grief is just a heavy silent presence, I try to figure out how to make everyone happy. I read books and listen to people who tell me what kind of wife I need to be for Taggart. What kind of friend I need to be. How I need to be to all these other people. I think that if I just make them happy, if I just stretch myself a little further, then I will finally earn their Love, and they will stay.

There's a feeling in me that I ignore when I think of them staying – of being able to one day know they will. The feeling is the opposite of Fear. It rises up in me warm, welcoming, like liquid gold. It's how I feel when I look at Taggart, but my knee jerk reaction is to be scared of it, because immediately after feeling it, Fear shows up. I've never known this feeling without Fear.

Sometimes I'm stretched so thin and juggle the balls of so many people's wants that I drop one. When this happens, I am sheer terror. I don't know which ball is more important. I don't know whose needs are more important, so I do what I've always done. I pay attention to the trouble and ignore the person who is making no demands of me. Taggart doesn't make demands. Actually, he does make one demand of me: he demands I take care of myself. I tell him that I am taking care of myself. How do I explain to him that when I am taking care of the needs of everyone else, it feels like I am taking care of me because I am earning the Love of the ones I love?

Fear tells me not to tell him. "He has so much on his plate, Emerson. It's your job to make his life easier, not harder."

I have a brief thought that if I was making his life easier, we wouldn't be in couples therapy, but Shame comes in and drowns out any other thought.

Taggart asks me about Grief. Dr. Q asks me about Grief, too. But Fear tells me that there's a time limit on how long I can tell people about Grief. That there are people who have it so much worse than me, and that Grief is not more important than what others are going through. That if I talk about Grief too much then I won't be taking care of their needs.

I believe Fear. After all, they've got lots of logic behind their reasoning.

When Grief comes to visit, I learn to retreat, to cope alone. My oldest friend, Frankie, who I've known longer than I've known Taggart, asks me about Grief. I tell her that I'm fine and we don't talk about it. She asks me about Charles. I shake my head and change the subject. I make a lot of jokes. Fear tells me that's the only acceptable way to reference Grief.

When I meet new people and they ask about my family, I don't know how to answer. I have lots of responses that come to mind.

"They're dead. Yes, all of them."

"I don't have one."

"They don't live nearby."

I never know how exactly to respond. When the question arises, Fear comes in and tells me to make a joke. Or ignore their question. Eventually I stop addressing it and turn the question back on them. Fear has made me really good at asking questions about other people.

"The key," Fear tells me over and over again. "Is to make other people feel like they know you, without actually knowing the real you."

"But isn't that a lie?"

"No," they remark. "Absolutely not. It's smart. No one wants to hear about your depressing story. You'll just make them sad."

Sometimes I ignore Fear, and I tell people straight to their face, "My family is dead."

I see the look on their face and the response is usually the same. "All of them?"

"Yes."

"You don't have any living family?"

"No."

At this, often eyes are filled. With tears. With pity. With horror. I rush in and explain to them that it's okay. I tell them I'm fine. I say "I'm fine" so often, I start to believe it. Even when there are follow up questions. And there are always have follow up questions.

"You lost your parents?"

"Yes."

"Both of them?"

"Yes."

"What about your siblings?"

"They died, too."

"How old were they when they died?"

"Charles was eighteen. Keating was twenty-six."

"They all died in the same year?"

"Yes."

"What about your grandparents? Cousins? Aunts? Uncles?"

"I don't have any."

"How did they all die?"

I opened this door, so I have to walk through it. And in doing so I hold their hand through my own Grief. This becomes hard for me. Too hard. So, I stop doing it altogether. I tell people I don't have siblings. This is the truth, even though I feel traitorous to my brothers' memories and then Fear makes me ask again.

"What if I forget them?"

I've learned to tell people that I don't talk with my family. I don't, so that's the truth. If people ask questions, I let Fear speak. I take on their way of talking – answering questions without actually answering. I deflect. I ask questions about the other person, and every time someone tells me they think I'm wonderful, Fear preens.

"See?" Fear says, brushing their glossy hair. "This is why we don't talk about you. You're not interesting."

I nod, agreeing.

Soon this is how I even operate at home. I don't talk to Taggart about Grief. If I have a bad day, I tell him I'm going to read or watch a movie and I silently sob into a pillow behind a shut door. I close my eyes and let the memories and the missing wash over me. I let Loss and Grief and Shame and Should come in, but I refuse to let Taggart in when they're here. And since they're here so often, I don't let Taggart in much at all. I do what I've always done; take care of myself, by myself.

Sometimes I talk to Frankie, but it's hard. Frankie has been around since I was nineteen. I forget that she knew them, too. She knew Charles. She knew the tumultuous relationship I had with my mom. She knew the pain that Keating inflicted upon me in the name of being his safe space. She knew Percy. She knew them all. When I talk to Frankie about it, she dispels Fear. Fear hates this.

"I don't like Frankie," Fear tells me over and over again.

"I don't care. I do."

Frankie is the only person I've ever met who can talk to my Fear.

"You can talk to me about these things. I *want* to know. I *want* to be here for you. I love you." She looks at me without judgement when she says these things, and I believe her.

But before I can open my mouth to share, Fear jumps in and makes a joke. Frankie calls Fear out for the joke. She sees the cloak that Grief wraps me in. But there is no couples therapy for best friends.

I have other friends. Great friends. But Frankie is the one who sees Fear and Grief, and even Shame and Should. She sees them, and though she doesn't judge me for them, she does address them. I don't feel as obligated to make sure that she's happy the way that I do with Taggart. She reminds me that Taggart loves me. She is honest with me even if it hurts. She's honest in the name of Love. There are so many times when I think that she has helped me so much and I haven't been as good a friend to her as she has been to me.

When I think this, Fear pops in and says, "You have to earn it. You have to do something that makes her see how deserving you are of this friendship."

I don't tell Frankie about Fear's comment. I don't tell anyone. I go to my office – the room I'm supposed to be using to work – and sit with Fear. I don't want them to call Loss, and I know that if I let Fear get too close to these relationships they will. Fear makes me mourn friendships and relationships that I haven't lost yet. This is their favorite thing to do.

"Why do I have to do this?" I say with my arms wrapped around my ever-growing stomach, trying to hold myself together.

"It's like training for a marathon. You have to be able to run the whole thing. You have to be prepared for the whole thing."

Fear pages through the catalogue of people I love, the people who've told me they loved me.

"Remember this one?"

Fear shows me the picture of the boy who made me weigh myself every morning. The one who didn't like when I wore red.

"Yes." My voice is small.

"He said he loved you."

"I know."

"It took you a long time to get past this."

"I know. I had Frankie though. She helped a lot."

"She did." Fear shows me how much I leaned on Frankie during this time. They show me that I didn't do my part to uphold my end of the friendship.

"Don't you think she's done enough? Do you really want to make her do this again? She can't help through this. No one can. You're on your own. That's the best way for you to handle it. On your own. You know how to do that. If you handle it on your own, you won't upset anyone else. And if you don't upset them then you're making them happy. Which, you might remember, is your job."

Fear tears a page out.

"Let's move on, okay?"

I nod. Fear is always right. I don't know them without Love. I don't know Love without Fear. I don't want to lose the ones I love. I don't want to lose their Love. I know there are things much worse than a broken wooden spoon over my butt, and I don't have the emotional or mental capacity to handle that.

Fear comes up with lots of contingency plans. They have files upon files of preparations in my mind. There's a file for what to do if

Taggart dies, a file for what to do if he cheats. There's a file for what to do if we get divorced. They even have a file for what to do if Frankie decides I'm too much. They have files for my other friends too. They have so many files for so many things that soon they're taking over my mind. It's claustrophobic. I don't know where to put all these files and they are taking up space. They're blocking all the light.

My mind feels too tight, like a sweater that has been shrunk in the dryer. Still, I wear it. I can't move my arms without feeling Fear. When Taggart hugs me and tells me he loves me, the sweater shrinks more. When I feel Grief around us and I don't have the space to go deal with it on my own, and Taggart has to watch Grief's torrent of emotions tear through me, the sweater shrinks even more and now my pants feel too tight, too.

Everything feels too tight. I want to breathe deeply, but I can only take shallow breaths. I want to acknowledge the Love I see on Taggart's face, in Frankie's embrace, but I can't acknowledge the Love without acknowledging the Fear. If Fear is the price I have to pay for Love, then I will. Because I can't imagine a life without Love. And because of this, I can't imagine a life without Fear.

Spring

The first bud of spring sings the other
seeds into joining her uprising.
– Amanda Gorman

Meditation

Quiet the mind and the soul will speak.
— Ma Jaya Sati Bhagavita

My mind has become a fucking free for all. I feel like a parent whose children got out of hand and no matter what I do, I can't rein them in. Fear, Grief, Shame, even Should come and go at all hours of the day and night, no regard for my own schedule. They invite friends over regardless of whether I need to concentrate or not. They have so many friends. Some are nondescript and seemingly neutral. Others are more chaotic, hyping them up to their strongest, most out of control selves.

I don't know what to do. I'm not in therapy anymore, but that doesn't mean the work stops simply because I stop writing a check out to the most expensive, most selfless friend I've ever had. I stopped going because there was nowhere either in my mind, or out of it, that I could go to gain the proper perspective without feeling attacked. The time had simply come where I needed to leave it, not dive further into it.

I need help. I need something more. I need God.

No one is more shocked by this epiphany than I am. Since Charles, I've been mad at God. Livid, even. I've stopped talking to Them. I've stopped listening. I can't rightly say I've stopped believing, though. I'm so confused. So angry. So scared. But I know if I feel these emotions toward God, then I still believe in something. What that something is, I don't know.

I had even gone to a Christian counselor before Dr. Q, searching for answers. I had taken care of Charles for so long, in so many confusing ways, and now with him beyond my reach, I thought it would make me feel better. But it doesn't make me feel better. It makes me feel worse.

I've never fully known how he died. I've only been told that he had simply never woken up. That was the beginning and the end of it. I had been the last phone call, the last one to show up, and there have been times that I've had this feeling in me that I can't explain - this knowing - that a decision had been made prior to contacting me, on what exactly I was to be told. A thousand images and ideas run through my head. Charles had taken the loss of our mother so hard. I wonder if he had committed suicide. He had been in constant contact with Keating who had been giving him "tips" on what drugs were best to mix. One of my final fights with Keating in fact, was me calling on Shame to berate Keating in my stead.

"You told him what?!" I screamed in horror.

"Don't worry about it, Emerson. Geez. I'm just helping him, so he knows what drugs are safe to use together."

"You know what drugs are 'safe' to use together, Keating? *No drugs!* He's eighteen - he just lost his mother, his father is already engaged to someone else, and he's spiraling. Be reasonable!"

Through his derisive laugh, Keating told me to chill. "He doesn't want to talk to you right now. He knows you're judging him. That's why he's talking to me. I got him a credit card. I'm helping him. I've got it under control."

I hung up, terrified, unable to do anything. For someone who has been told her whole life that it was her job to make everyone else happy, to put everyone else's needs first, this was a real mind-fuck.

Shame loves that scene so much. He constantly plays it, even after

Keating dies. He tries to get me to vilify Keating, but I can't. I've always known who Keating was, and even if it didn't make sense to me, he really was just trying to help Charles the best way he knew how. I can't find it in me to be mad at him. He had been mad enough at himself for a lifetime.

This is why I need God. This is why I need someone – *something* – that's bigger than me. Something that is *more*. I need something that will help me to fill the voids I don't even know are there. This is why I scoop up all of my broken parts, hold them in my hands, and beg.

I talk with Betty, my Christian counselor asking where she thinks Charles is. She tells me that she doesn't know; that no one really knows. I tell her all I can see is that scene from the movie What Dreams May Come where Robin Williams goes to Hell to rescue his wife and bring her to Heaven.

I can't stop seeing that scene. That entire movie, actually, where he decides to plant himself in Hell with her if he can't bring her out, knowing that for him, Heaven wouldn't actually be Heaven without her.

I can't go to Hell, though. Or Heaven for that matter. As much space as Grief, Fear, Depression, and Shame take up, I don't want to die. I don't really know how to live right now, but I do know that I'm not the only one left standing for nothing. So, when Loss skirts the edges of my vision, I remember the promise I made that I would fight her.

With all that in mind, I go to the places that have always been my church - bookstores. I walk around them seemingly aimless. I pray in them, if you can call it that. I ask God to lead me to the books I need to read. I tell God that I don't care what the books are about. I ask God for signs. And when I can't bring myself to talk to God anymore, I talk to my mom. She was the one who had instilled such a deep, abiding love of books in me. So here in the bookstores, when I feel confused about God, I reach for my mother. I even smell her perfume, though no one is around.

I find that I am drawn to certain books. Some for no reason that I can ascertain until months after I read them. With others the reason is so clear that I laugh right there in the store. I download a library app and read on my phone until my bleary eyes can't handle anymore.

I discover Meditation from about a billion different books. I read *Eat Pray Love* like everyone else and find that *Pray* is the chapter I love the most. I read other books; books that mention Meditation in all sorts of different ways. I become a bit overwhelmed. I sign up for an at home Meditation challenge from Deepak Chopra and Oprah. I can't stick to it though. They want me to write about my Meditations. They want me to use a mantra. I try and try though it's not working. I begin to worry that it won't.

I try sitting with my legs crossed. I try sitting in the grass. I call Meditation over and over and over again, begging her to show up and help. Begging her to fit in my life. If Meditation were a person, I would be the recipient of many a restraining order.

It sounds troubling, I know. But my mind doesn't feel like my own. I don't feel like I belong to myself. And for me, though this isn't a last-ditch effort, it does feel like I'm in the middle of that emergency search and rescue. Only I'm calling Mediation instead of 911. There's a feeling in me, a nudging from the inside that if I just keep calling, if I just keep trying, she'll show up. And one day, despite the barrage of clutter and noise in my mind, she does.

I'm lying on my bed, desperate for a reprieve. I feel like I've run a mental marathon just that morning, and though ill equipped, I'm gearing up for another one. I put on classical music. Chopin, I believe. It soothes me. I lay on my bed, arms out, palms up. My head cushioned between Taggart's stack of pillows and my own in a cozy attempt for silence. I stare at the ceiling, until my eyelids became so heavy, they drift shut of their own accord. I don't know what to ask for. I don't have a mantra. I don't have any words. I just shove all my feelings toward where I think God might be. Toward where I hope my family is. And I stare into the dark.

It feels almost like I'm asleep, but I know I'm not. There's an awareness. I'm not alone, but the negative emotions aren't there, either.

"Hello?" A voice that both is and isn't mine echoes through the space. It should feel empty. It should feel lonely. It doesn't.

"Hello, Emerson."

Cool hands reach out for mine, softly reassuring, smelling of light and wonder. "It's wonderful to finally meet you."

Sparkling tears drip from my eyes. "Are you...is this?"

She smiles at me, so bright, so serene. "Yes. I'm Meditation."

I look around, straining to see. Straining to hear.

"It's so peaceful here."

Tucking my hand in the crook of her arm, she begins to walk with me. "Thank you. I'm quite fond of it." Leading us to a set of chairs, luxurious in their simplicity, we both sit. "You were starting to worry."

"Yes," I pause here waiting for Shame to show up.

"He can't come here."

"He can't?"

"No," she says, a glow of light around her.

"Are you God, too?" I feel like a child just learning to read.

A bell-like laugh washes over me. "What a wonderful question. Such curiosity."

We sit for a while in companionable silence.

"What kind of meditation is this?"

She lifts an elegant shoulder. "That doesn't matter."

"It doesn't?"

Leaning toward me, I catch a bit of her scent. I can't place it, but I'm instantly at ease. It's bright yet soft. Her voice is both a sound and a feeling, and something I don't think there is a name for.

"No, Emerson. It doesn't matter how you got here. Only that you did."

I begin to apologize for constantly harassing her, but her laugh tinkles out again. "I started wondering if my mind was too loud, too busy for you."

"No need for apologies, my love. Those are the exact sort of minds that need me most. Now tell me, what can I do for you?"

I spill everything. I tell her the story that she already knows. I tell her that I need an overhaul. I tell her I need to get control of my mind back.

"Mmmmm." A long finger taps her full mouth. "Did you ever have control?"

She asks this without judgement, her voice neutral in its sincerity. I don't have an answer. I'm not meant to.

I'm propelled out of Meditation and back into my bed, in my room, in the home I share with my husband. I touch myself to see if I'm real and laugh a bit maniacally. I wait for Shame, for Should, even Grief. But they don't come. I wait for Fear, but even they are nowhere to be found.

I feel lighter. I feel quieter. I feel full of liquid gold.

This is how I return to Meditation for a long time. I lay in my bed, arms out, staring into the void behind closed eyelids. I realize over time that Meditation is not just a feeling, it's a place. And I can both go there and be with her simultaneously.

We build a relationship based on nothing and everything. She knows everything and she judges nothing. My mind is quiet when I leave her, and when the Others try to come, it's as though they're behind a nearly soundproof wall. Their voices are indistinct, and the claustrophobia that accompanies them is lifted. It doesn't matter that this sometimes only lasts for minutes and sometimes lasts for days. I'm just grateful that it's happening at all.

There are days where I struggle on my way to Meditation. On those days, Should is particularly loud.

"You should be able to do this effortlessly by now." She watches me, judging, from the corner of my mind she has planted herself in.

"I don't think anything is 'effortless', Should," I tell her, getting sucked into the conversation. Bearing down, sweat beads on my brow until I rise, defeated. This happens sometimes. Usually when I need Meditation most.

Sometimes, when I am with Meditation, I ask questions. I have a lot of questions for her, about her.

"Where are we? Where is this?" I ask this a lot, never satisfied with the answer.

"We are." She always replies. Simply. Exasperatingly.

"Have we left my mind? Or are we still in it?"

"Yes." She always says, answering both questions in a way that I can understand only when I am with her.

After some time, I begin to understand that the place is in me. I am in my mind and away from it. I have left and gone to a part of it that is rarely used, that is accessible by a door that only I have the key to. And one day, I'm sitting at my computer, staring out the window above my desk, when something happens. Meditation comes to me with my hands hovering above the keys, and my eyes closed. Something rises in me, and trusting that, I lay my hands on the keys, open a new document and begin to type.

Close your eyes. Count to ten. Inhale deeply through your nose with your face lifted to the sky. Count to three. Exhale through your mouth until your shoulders drop and your face tilts slightly downward. Release your thoughts with every iota of breath you exhale. Do this until your mind is empty. I know, an empty mind seems impossible. If you are struggling, imagine your thoughts as strings of words. Use your imagination to grab the tail end of each sentence, connect it to your mouth, and imagine your breath is the sentence or thought. Expel it from you. When you blow your breath out, the letters will jumble and float off into the world, to create happier thoughts for others. Do this until each sentence or thought is released and your mind is empty. You don't have to lie down. You don't have to move. Your mind is empty. You have created a safe space for yourself by doing this. You have created a space to return to when you need to be alone. Imagine yourself now sitting in the space your thoughts have just vacated. What does it look like? Mine is an empty room. Windowless. Gray. I'm sitting bathed in light, in a lotus position, though I do not enjoy this position in physical form. My hands are resting on my folded knees, my eyes closed. The room is curved, because I am in my brain. It is gray, and windowless, though the light circles me like a spotlight. This is the light I bathe myself in. This is the light I let myself be bathed in. I don't ask where it comes from or how it got into a windowless space. I am both the receiver of light and the light itself. This light is safe. It is free of temperature. It is joy. It is calm. It is bright. It is comforting. It is everything. If I move, the light moves because the light is both of me and for me. This is how I reset myself. I can stay here as long as I need to because I am always here. The room is small, but not confining. I can make the room bigger if I need to, but I don't need to. I am cocooned in love. I am both of the love and the receiver of love. I see my spirit leave the physical image I have of myself sitting in the room and walk. Sometimes she paces. Sometimes she simply walks the perimeter. The light stays on my physical image and my spirit, while physically unconnected, feels everything the light feels. I am the light. This is my soul, walking. She doesn't always look like me. Sometimes she is older. Sometimes she is younger. They are all me. I am all them. Sometimes I ask them to sit with me, and they do. They circle around me, at the edge of the room lining the curve. Sometimes there are more, yet the room never changes. They are respectful to the light. They mirror my position when I invite them into the room. When I smile, they smile. When I open my eyes, they are looking at me. They are me. I am they. This is me, sitting with myselves. We are all there because we are not there at all. When I realize this, the room is empty again, but for my physical image in the center. This never moves. Perhaps THIS is the spirit. I cannot make out their face, for there is none. There is simply a sense of a feeling I cannot name. The closest I can come is joy, but that feels inaccurate. This sense is so far above joy, joy seems a slight. The light is no longer coming from the top of the room. The light is now in me. I am the light. I am the light until I am not the physical image and all that is left is light.

I open my eyes. I don't read what I've written. I know that I have created a guide for myself when I struggle to get to Meditation. Closing my eyes, I return to Meditation, to the room, and feeling wholly undivided, here in my desk chair I fall deeper.

Meditation, I realize, is not simply a place, it's a choice. Meditation is so many things I have no name for. Each time I leave, I feel both restored and safe. I carry that into my daily life.

After years of consistent silence and solace, Meditation has chosen this moment to shift. No longer am I simply silencing my Grief, escaping my Fear, exiling Shame. In that space when I am with the versions of myself, I realize that these versions; the ones I've been, the ones I've yet to be; are all me. And I have a duty to them, an obligation, to care for them.

"You see, don't you." It's not a question.

"Yes."

She and I are back in the room, all the versions of myself surrounding us. She asks me to choose one. Feeling a nudge that is neither her nor me, I am guided to one.

I sense her smile, and she brings me further into her fold. We travel together to my childhood bedroom during ages twelve to fifteen. Meditation and I sit on the bed. I see younger Emerson sitting on the floor listening to music, writing in a notebook. I feel her. Her loneliness. Her uncertainty. She looks up as if she knows I am there, but she can't see me. I am a feeling, not something that can be seen.

I remember this moment. I remember how perplexing and obsolete everything became this year; the year that things evolved into the way they would always be.

"What are we doing here?" I ask Meditation, whispering so younger Emerson couldn't hear.

"We're sitting with her. She's very isolated. She needs you."

Meditation eases off the bed, moving to wrap her arms around young Emerson.

I see the younger version of me look up, hope and longing evident on her face. She closes her eyes, and with a smile that speaks of solace, draws in a deep breath.

"Time to go."

Meditation and I return to consciousness.

"What the hell was that?" Running to a mirror, I check my

reflection. "I'm not that young girl anymore, but was – was I sitting with her?"

"Yes," Meditation answers calmly.

"Why was I sitting with her? Is that even possible? Am I going insane?"

I hurl questions at her, Should rising in my throat. Something inside me, warm and bright rises up, eliminating Should, nudging me to breathe.

"You're not insane, Emerson. So many things are possible that you aren't even aware of yet."

"But you didn't answer my question. Why were we with her? With me?" I cock my head. "Which is correct?"

Meditation shrugs. "Both. Either."

"So, why?"

"You'll see."

This begins to happen more and more often. Sometimes with Meditation we stay in the space of ease and serenity. Sometimes we travel to sit with myself at a different age. We never speak to Young Emerson. We never reveal ourselves. We just sit holding whatever version I have been guided to, in silence.

After a while, it dawns on me that we are offering comfort and connection to myself at certain times. Times I would later see in Shame's seemingly never-ending catalogue. Times I was taught to listen to Should. Times when Depression began to lurk in corners, and Loss showed up as gaps in both memory and relationships. Times when Fear had been used as a tool, as logic, as both defender and weapon.

At one particularly dark moment, I find it difficult to sit by and do nothing. Young Emerson is baffled, unsure what's going on, being pulled in every direction. She's unable to focus on her own needs. She's unsure if she's even allowed to.

"Can I do something to help? Is that permitted?"

Meditation's response is infuriating. "You tell me."

I am incredibly young in this moment that we have traveled back to. It's a time I can't consciously recall, due to both age and a gap in memory that Loss had taken. It is a moment that Shame would play on his screen for years to come, shrouding me in his sick darkness. It is where Fear's inception begins in earnest. I can't feel them here, but I can see that this younger version of me can. What I can feel is that inexplicable nudge, and following it, I reach deeper into Meditation.

There.

My hand brushes a pocket of light; warm, steady, encouraging.

I plant it in the corner of Young Emerson's subconscious. Looking to Meditation, she smiles and the whole space glows with the knowing that I cannot explain.

For years to come, in each Meditation with any of my younger selves, I water it; that pocket of light; with a Love I can't explain, and watch it grow.

"Do you know what that light is? Do you know what it's called, Emerson?"

Meditation's glow emanates until it not only encompasses my subconscious, but my entire being.

"It's light. It was so blindingly dark," I begin, a bit bewildered. "I wanted her to be able to see."

Meditation clasps my hands in hers, eyes streaming, radiating the Love I don't understand.

"That light is your Intuition. You followed it. You knew where to find it, where to plant it, what to feed it. You watered it. You Loved it. And now," She kisses my face, wet with my own tears. "Now, my darling, you're ready to meet it."

Meditation gestures to a previously unseen doorway. "Go on. She's waiting for you."

Intuition

For the spiritual being, intuition is far more than a hunch. It is viewed as guidance or as God talking, and this inner insight is never taken lightly or ignored.
– Wayne Dyer

I walk through the doorway and into a space that instantly felt both familiar and right.

"I know this place," I murmur to myself.

"Of course, you do."

I know that voice, too. I've heard it all my life. With the realization that it had been here all my life, the sensation rose up inside me, so bright, so warm. Like honey in my veins. Like my mother's butterscotch voice reading to me as a child.

I breathe in the familiar scent of it. Vanilla. Lilacs on Easter. Autumn leaves tingeing the air. The magic of snow on Christmas morning. It smells like all my favorite memories, all my favorite things rolled into one. It is a clear night with all the stars bright and shining. It is falling in Love.

"I know you." Focusing on the nudging inside me, and now all around me, I know that I'm finally meeting the thing that has saved me more times than I can count. "I've followed you a few times."

"You certainly have. More than you think, I daresay."

"You're a voice, yes, but it feels more like a nudging — like an inexplicable understanding of what's right. I could never explain that before. That knowing. I much prefer the knowing to being told what to do."

An image of Should flashes in front of my eyes, but I shake my head to get rid of it.

"I really don't care to be told what to do."

A feeling akin to a laugh bubbling up in my chest envelopes me.

"Oh, I don't tell you what to do. I simply show pathways. In very much the same way you can choose to call upon Meditation, you can choose to follow my knowing."

Her voice brings to mind a dewy meadow in spring. I'm a child running across barefoot, so fast and so free that my feet barely touch the earth. I lay down in the grass, but now it's a pillowy cloud, cushioning me as I float through the sky, giggling uproariously. I point out a cloud that looks like a giant, silly hat. Then one that is a silly, clumsy dog, its ears flapping in the wind. Still another is a sinuous mermaid, diving in the air around me, playfully blowing a breeze that kisses my cherubic cheeks.

I've never been so full of faith, or rightness. I've never felt so safe, so certain that this is a place that is just for me; to protect me, to love me, to encircle me. I want to live in this doorway. I want to follow it, wherever it leads.

"Open your eyes, Emerson."

"I can't quite visualize you...." I concentrate harder. "You're more of an impression than an image."

"Mmmm. Shall we sit?"

Lowering myself to the sofa that resembles the one in my own living room I feel overcome. Unable, or unwilling to repress the laughter that pours from me, I choose to embrace it.

"What are you called? I know you're my Intuition. I must have given you a name. I do so love to name things."

Her gaze rests on me, softly reassuring. Almost maternal. For a moment I think I see my own mother's face, smell her signature perfume. I am overcome with a Love I don't understand.

"You already know it. Let's just sit with one another and see what comes to mind, hmmm?" Drawing a cup and saucer from the coffee table, she is the picture of patience.

I feel her smile as she lifts the teacup to her lips. Shrugging, I lean back and close my eyes. I'll drop in on Meditation.

"You don't have to tell me anything," Meditation silences me. "I know what you're looking for. Intuition is with you, so allow her to guide you where you need to go. Oh, and Emerson, dear? Keep an open mind."

Before I can remark, I am propelled back. It's as though my life is flashing before my eyes, each moment a continuance of the one before and the one after.

Everything was supposed to happen this way, everything was supposed to lead me here.

A song plays around me like a breeze. It's a song that has been a favorite of mine for years. It's so sad but I have always found it so comforting in my own moments of sadness. Moments, I realize now, where I had come back to water the light I had planted.

A movie, so terribly upsetting I sobbed when I watched it, but watched it over and over. I found reassurance in this movie and others like it. I was drawn to these dark films that, unbeknownst to me, were preparing me for Depression and Loss.

A color I wore so often because my mother told me it made my eyes stand out.

A flower I've always been obsessed with.

A character in a movie I identify with.

So many flashes before me. I almost can't keep up. Tiny moments. Huge moments. And I pluck the name out of not thin air, but memory.

"Iris." I said aloud. "Your name is Iris."

"So it is, my love. And a good one at that." A sunbeam of warmth came from inside me.

"Iris. You've been with me for so long," my eyes widen in shock. "You were there the first time I saw Taggart."

"Yes."

That moment is almost seared into my brain. Frankie and I had been doing some holiday shopping. She had been on the phone and suddenly, Taggart walked into the store. I remember clearly, he had been wearing a Christmas red sweater. He was with a friend, and as he walked past me, we had made eye contact. A rush of recognition had washed over me, inside me, and when I turned around for another look, he had too. Everything had softened, but his face, in clear, bright, crystalline focus.

Iris and I sit for what seems like hours and talk. We talk about all the times she was there, and I didn't know it. All the times she was there and I did. All the times I had a feeling of what I needed to do or needed to avoid.

"All those nudges that I felt that I listened to - those were you. I could never explain it –" I shake my head. "How could I ever explain this? How are you even here? Like this, I mean?"

The light that she is, that is in me, is so bright, so warm, so full of rightness that I think I might burst apart.

"I don't understand."

"Yes, you do. Feel me. Feel." She places her palm on my abdomen. "This is where you feel me. Feel me now, Emerson. I'm simply your Intuition. I will only ever love you and take care of you. You've only to trust me. You've only to believe in me."

"But if you're in me, then that means I have to trust in myself? I have to believe in myself?"

"Yes, you do. But if you trust me first, I will help you with the rest. You are so loved, my darling. You are so cherished. And all I want is to be here with you and to help you." Hands like sunrise over dew reach for my face. I lean my cheek into them.

As the weeks wear on, I discover something interesting. Though I discovered Iris because of Meditation, I don't need Meditation to continue my relationship with her. On the contrary, I feel Iris all the time. And those days I struggled with Meditation? They're nearly nonexistent. The closer I get to Iris, the more I pay attention to her, the more surreally peaceful my time with Meditation is.

In fact, when Grief hulls me out, when Shame makes me cringe, when Depression's haze rolls in, when Fear creates a tunnel of claustrophobia, I can always find the golden warmth that is Iris. She's quiet, but constant. She offers the strength and conviction to me that I had offered to her in each visit with Meditation. In taking care of her, I take care of me. And in letting her be there for me, I am there for her.

"I've read a lot about Meditation. It seems you two are pretty close," I remark one day, as I read a book that mentions her.

"We are," her words a song.

"Yet you're able to come to me, the way Grief does, the way Shame does. You rise up in me the way Fear does. I have to seek out Meditation."

Putting my book aside, I focus on her. "I'm having a hard time finding books on you, though. Oh, you're mentioned here and there, and alluded to more often than not. Don't get me wrong, working with Meditation taught me the importance of understanding that what is right for some isn't right for others. I understand that. I just … I'd like to know more about you. I feel like there's more to you."

Iris hums a little note as she thinks. I can almost feel myself knowing what she's going to say before she says it, as she translates from feeling to language. I still need her to tell me though.

"You've read a lot about Meditation, Emerson. You know that praying is talking to God, and a great many people do this. Even more do this without realizing that's what they're doing. There were times when you didn't know what to pray for, what to verbalize, so what did you do?"

"I pushed all my feelings toward where I felt God was. I figured They would be able to figure it out."

Nodding at me, she continues. "Yes. You've also read that Meditation is the act of listening to God. That those who wish for answers to their many questions often use Meditation to try to obtain those answers. Sometimes they do obtain those answers. Sometimes they don't; instead finding a delightful fulfillment that requires no answer that anyone else could possibly understand. Through Meditation, you yourself have experienced so much comfort, so much serenity. You've been introduced to other parts of yourself. You've stretched your capacity for not only knowledge, but Empathy, Compassion. You've become someone who chooses —"

"Chooses what?"

"Anything. You've chosen to look inward and evolve, to look at what's happened to you and rather than escape it, you've asked for more. More knowledge, more understanding, more purpose. And so, in asking, God has given it to you. You chose to help your younger self in that darkness; to leave lanterns for her to find to help guide her out, knowing that the path would still be quite rigorous."

Embarrassed now, I mutter, "I couldn't just leave her there without tools, Iris."

An iridescent tear trails down her cheek. "No, my darling. *You* could not have. But you chose. And you choose, every day, to climb rather than succumb."

"No, Iris. I caved. Loss came for my sense of self before, and I gave it willingly. Depression came, and I let them stay. Shame came, and I stopped fighting him. Fear wove themself into the fabric of who I am, and I allowed it. And Death," Grief tries to rip the words from my throat. "Death took what he wanted. Because of that, I'm saddled with Grief for the rest of my life."

Iris lets me feel all my feelings without judgement or reproach. She rocks me, like a nurturing mother. Her arms like cashmere roped around me, the silky wonder of her Love deep, like an October night.

"Do you know why Meditation and I are such good friends?"

"No," I hiccup, wiping my nose with my sleeve like a child. "Why?"

"Meditation is the act of listening to God. I am the answer."

"But...that means ..."

"Mmmm." Quietly confident she continues to rock me.

"That means that – you're the voice of God? I don't understand."

She places her hand on my abdomen.

"You don't understand me with logic. Here. Feel."

I place my hand over hers. The golden radiance of her lights me up from the inside out. I feel a stretch of knowing unfurl itself and rise up my spine. Something close to an orgasm encapsulates every cell of my body, coalescing up my backbone through the crown of my head where I feel a tingling, a pulling. A shudder ripples through me. Only the cool, tingling tethers remains.

"It feels like the color blue. Can I feel the color blue?"

"You tell me."

"Yes. I *can* feel the color blue. But not a dark blue. It's bright, almost neon, but less harsh. More of a glow. Like lightning at night. But cool, refreshing, like a freshwater stream." Eyes closed; I place my other hand on my center.

"Incandescent. The word is incandescent."

"What else do you feel?"

"I feel a bit dizzy, like I'm not actually anchored here. I feel like my body is just weight. Just a thing. A tool. I don't actually live in my body, Iris."

"Where do you live, Emerson, darling?"

My arms open wide. "I live everywhere. I'm energy. I'm spirit. I'm here for a reason. You're here because I asked for answers to my questions. You're the answer to the questions."

I open my eyes, staring at her with the Love I am just beginning to comprehend. She looks like me now. I reach out and grab my own hands, feeling Iris. Feeling myself.

"You're in me," I said. "You're here to help me heal."

"Yes, darling. I am."

I hug myself. The tingling in the center at the top of my skull radiates down, engulfing me in what can only be called pure rightness.

"Everyone has Intuition. It's what is quiet and sure when everything else is loud." A quote from a book flashes into my mind and comes out of my mouth. "God dwells in you, as you."

I see now. I see with eyes that belong to both me and Iris.

"If God dwells in me, as me, then you, my Intuition, you're the God in me."

I feel her yes sweep through me so strongly. It rings in me, beaming - intertwining her gold with the blue.

"I feel God, Iris. They love us so much. They don't care how we love Them. They just care that we do."

She brushes her hands across my cheeks.

"We just want you to let us love you. Let us love you, Emerson."

Iris and I sit, and just as I'm about to become one with Iris, Should creeps, telling me I shouldn't be able to talk to God. Let alone hear Them. Let alone *house* them.

I try to reason with her. I explain that everyone has Intuition. I explain that Iris has always been here inside me, and that I've listened to her before, so I don't understand what the big fuss is now.

"Emerson, I'm here to try to help you," Should pleads with me. "Look at the rest of the world. There aren't people having conversations with themselves outside of padded rooms. You should listen to *me*. You shouldn't listen to Iris. She shouldn't be so tangible to you. This is what happens to crazy people." Should tries to call out for Shame, for Grief, for Depression, for Loss. She cries out for Fear, demanding they do their job.

"Someone help me with her. This shouldn't be happening!"

"Should," I began, staring into her overwrought eyes. "I know what I'm doing. It's alright."

Iris guides me to a metal plate with an attached knob. On the plate are two words. 'Should: Volume'

Somehow, I know I can't mute her completely. Not yet. I lower her volume as far as I can and watch with pity as her eyes go wide with shock and entitlement.

"You shouldn't be able to do that." It comes out in a whisper.

Iris holds my hand and knowing permeates through my entire being.

"This is just the beginning, isn't it?" I say. "There's a lot of work ahead of me."

"Yes, my dear. There is." She pushes a lock of hair out of my eyes.

"You'll help me." It isn't a question. She answers anyway.

"Yes."

Reframing

When any real progress is made, we unlearn and
learn anew what we thought we knew before.
– Henry David Thoreau

"Emerson, darling."

"Hmm?" I'm with Meditation and Iris. Over the last few months, they've become my closest companions and confidants.

Iris is walking around. She does that quite often. I usually just let her roam. She knows her way around. And I trust her.

"Darling, I wonder if you'd let me run an idea past you. Meditation, dear," she continues. "Would you mind terribly if I had some time alone with Emerson?"

Meditation rises from her position on the ground. "Not at all. I imagine I'll see you soon."

She winks at me. I see Grief tapping his foot impatiently, waiting for the rest of his party to show up. I still can't quite rein the Others in, but my connection with Iris helps me from feeling too overwhelmed. Most of the time.

Even now, hand in hand, we meander around the space that Grief occupies. I'm able to notice things I didn't before. His space is messy and dark. He doesn't really pick up after himself and likes to leave bits scattered everywhere.

"Emerson," Iris began again. "I wonder if you'd - pardon the pun - mind some renovations. You know, continue that overhaul."

"Renovations? More of them?"

"Well, yes. It's really incredibly outdated in here. I think we'd both feel a bit better, now that we've gotten so close. Update it a bit - create a safer space, bring in more light, organize."

Thoughtfully tapping my finger to my lips, I glance around. It does feel dark and incredibly claustrophobic.

Before I can give my consent to a mindful renovation, Grief takes over. His friends have arrived, and his party is in full swing. I can still feel Iris, but Grief is acting like a recalcitrant child, stubbornly demanding attention. Should comes in with Shame hot on her heels, indignant I've spent any amount of time enjoying myself without a thought of my mother, of Charles, of Keating. They take over for a few days, and though I know Iris is there, I know that she won't do anything without my consent.

"Enough!" It bellows out of me, and grasping for Iris, I urge her. "Yes. Do it."

Through the chatter of the Others, I hear the insistent ringing of a doorbell.

Annoyed at yet another uninvited guest, I cover my ears. "I don't even *have* a doorbell!"

"Sure, you do." Dancing toward one of the longstanding walls, Iris throws open a door.

My brow crinkles. "I didn't know there was a door there."

She winks at me. "Emerson, if *I* know, *you* know."

Rather than feeling chastised, I feel almost serene at the reminder. "Oh, yeah. Who is it?"

A short, balding man sporting a hard hat, tool belt, and the rosiest cheeks I've ever seen outside a Christmas movie saunters in. I like him immediately.

"Oy! How ya doin'?" He looks from me to Iris. "Someone call for some Reframing?"

I bolt over to him. "Yes, I did. Thank you for coming."

He glances around warily, taking in the party. His presence has caused a lot of guests to leave, but the Others stubbornly remain.

"This is some place," the little old man who calls himself Reframing whistles.

Should yanks my shoulder, hissing in my ear. "You shouldn't have called him. He hates it. He should leave. You shouldn't need help - you should be able to do this on your own."

In my attempt to flick her off, I draw Reframing's attention.

"Alright, lemme see whatcha got."

He walks up to Should, measuring her with a funny looking measuring tape I've never seen before.

"What does…"

Iris approaches, offering a soothing lavender pressure on my arm. "Let's let him assess the situation."

We watch as the adorable little man walks around my mind. He knocks on beams. He kicks walls. He weaves around the endless stacks of files. He uses a funny little thing to test the air, and, like Inspector Gadget, grows taller to check what he calls, 'the ceiling'. Finally, after crawling under the foundation, he swaggers up to Grief.

Grief, with no friends left, resembles a cocky teenager who clearly has a problem with authority.

"What are you looking at?" Grief takes a draw on a cigarette. I think he got it from Shame.

Reframing sniffs the smoke, his white mustache twitching.

"Ah." He scribbles something on his clipboard, and the longer he stands there, the more Grief evolves into an adult.

I find the exchange amusing. Grief's had run of the place for so long that he almost blends in with the curtains.

Reframing continues to write on the clipboard with one hand, while the other holds the measuring tape that he used with Should.

"Okay." He clicks it and snaps it back into his tool belt. Gesturing with his thumb, he walks to a corner Grief doesn't often go.

"Would you like to sit down?" I ask, indicating the table and chairs beside us. He nods once in answer to my question and drops heavily into a chair.

He puts his clipboard and his tape measure on the table. I go to pick it up, curious, but Iris shakes her head at me.

"Alright," his voice is gruff, sandpapery. "It's good you called me. It's definitely dated and if you hadn't had Iris here," he wags a thumb at her. "You'd have had even more serious structural damage. She bought you a couple years, but really, it's just a matter of time. I can help you, but your foundation's shot."

Before I can say anything, I'm filled with Iris' calm knowing.

"Look kid, it's not your fault. Foundation work is delicate business. Whoever installed yours," he shoots me a sympathetic look, and noting my defensive posture, starts his sentence again. "I know whoever installed yours isn't around anymore."

He checks his clipboard, scratching his chin.

"Usually, I prefer to work with the ones that installed it since they know the ins and outs, but in this case, we don't have that option. If you leave it the way it is, it's all gonna crumble and if that happens, it's gonna take everything that you built down with it. I need to bring in a foundation expert. I can't do this on my own."

I'm not surprised. I don't need Iris to tell me that this is essential. Reframing certainly isn't the first to point out my foundation issues. I remember Dr. Q talking about them, using words like 'abuse' and 'gaslighting'. I didn't want to hear them then, and though I don't particularly want to hear them now, I can't deny the truth in Reframing's words.

Sighing heavily, I say. "Let's do it."

Grabbing the pencil from behind his ear, he pulls out a calculator and starts pushing buttons. "Okay, so here's an estimate on how much it's gonna cost."

I attempt to decipher his calculations, but I can't understand them. "In what?"

"Time. Energy. You put both of those in with me so you can get more down the road. We're gonna create a better space together, kid.

You're gonna love it." His calloused hand reaches out to shake mine. "Let's get started."

The moment I drop his hand, Reframing puts his pinky fingers in his mouth and lets out a piercing whistle.

Utterly charmed by him, I find myself asking. "And that's for...?"

He looks back at me on his way to the door. "My partner. I told you, I need an expert."

The door opens to a tall lithe woman, beautifully clad in a tailored suit the color of ripe raspberries. Her hand, freshly manicured, thrust delicately toward me.

"Hi, Emerson." Her handshake is brisk and graceful; like her. "I'm Unlearning. Let's go check out this foundation."

Reframing pulls her into a hug. "Damn good to see you again, Unlearning."

She tips his hardhat playfully. "Got another one of those for me?"

"You bet."

They spend a few days walking around, muttering and laughing like the old friends I can tell they are. When they're not walking around, they're watching me. They're crawling under the floorboards, checking the ceiling, making notes, speaking in the language reserved for those who've known each other for years. Grief has been noticeably absent since Reframing's shown up. I think he scared him off. Maybe that's his job.

After they're there for a while, I stop noticing them. I go about my life, business as usual. A few weeks later, on a sunny spring day, I'm outside walking when something reminds me of my mother. I don't know what it is, but I catch a whiff that takes me back. Shame saunters in, flanked by Should and Grief.

Before I know it, I'm overcome with the immensity of Grief's presence. He's pulled me into him. Somehow Shame has also started a reel and Should flicks her wrist to spread out a blanket. My stomach hits the floor as realization dawns. They're not planning on leaving anytime soon.

Shame starts his routine, and even though I know what to expect, I'm never prepared for it. The reel starts.

Where is Iris? I scream inside my head. My breathing starts to hitch, and I feel the sharp stab of darkness spread out, upending the floor beneath me. I barely notice. That's not what I'm paying attention to.

Out of the corner of my eye, I see Reframing and Unlearning approach stealthily. Reframing grabs Grief. Unlearning wrangles both Shame and Should. She hauls them off to the center of my mind where she shines a spotlight on them both. Should preens a little. She likes being the center of attention. Shame, preferring the sticky secret dark, recoils.

Unlearning watches them for a while, letting them seethe. Reframing has gone to his toolbox and before he grabs anything, I notice his hands are on his knees. He's stretching. I watch mesmerized, when he abruptly stands and begins to move around my mind. He checks his clipboard, knocking on walls and beams. He mutters to himself, marking them with chalk.

"Hollow. That's what I thought. Structural, my ass."

He's chewing on a piece of dried lavender, which I find mildly amusing. When he catches me watching him, he winks, then nods to Unlearning.

"You ready to do this?"

Still in shock at the quick turn of events, I see her return his nod. Iris is vibrating inside me with knowing.

Unlearning is correcting Shame and Should on their rights. Apparently, they don't have any.

"Are you arresting them?" My voice is thready as I watch two of the bullies in my life cower beneath Unlearning's gaze.

"Yes. I am."

She's strong. Poised. She clearly intimidates them. I find myself even more intrigued.

"Shall we have a chat?"

Should raises a manicured finger. "I shouldn't be here. I didn't do anything wrong."

She smiles a perfect smile, straight white teeth sparkling, not a hair out of place.

Unlearning completely ignores Should, gaze locked with Shame. Shame stares back, his black eyes boring into Unlearning's bright blue ones.

"I believe your time has come, Shame. Gather your things. You're finished here."

"The fuck I am," Shame hisses. "I go where I want, when I want. Besides, she likes it."

He looks past Unlearning, trying to find my eyes, but she moves in front of me, blocking me from his view.

"That's precisely what I thought you'd say."

Unlearning turns to face me, and she is all I see. I can't see my Shame behind her, or the face Should shows me.

"Emerson." Her hands rest on my shoulders. Confident. Sure. Gentle. "You are allowed to love Percy."

The wind is knocked out of me. I vaguely register Shame rattling his cuffs.

She begins to talk to me, her voice soothing and accepting. She tells me that Love is never wrong.

"You were the child, Emerson. It wasn't your job to take care of Keating. You loved both Keating *and* Percy. You don't have to choose. Loving Percy doesn't mean you *didn't* love Keating."

I'm incredibly uncomfortable. This is a new sensation, and I don't know how I feel about it. Iris unfurls inside me, and while I trust her, I feel like I'm learning a foreign language.

Behind me, I hear Reframing wielding a sledgehammer. He's knocking down walls.

"But…"

"Emerson, listen to me. It is not your fault that Charles died. It is not your fault that Keating killed himself. It is not your responsibility to make sure that everyone else comes before you. You are allowed to come first. Do you hear me? You matter. You are allowed to come first."

I nod slowly, unshed tears blurring my vision, a knot in my throat.

We sit like this for weeks as I let the information sink in, Unlearning repeating it over and over until it replaces what I have believed for so many years.

Shame is pissed. I can feel it. Should is shaking her head, saying 'no' over and over again.

"You don't have to apologize for loving anyone," Unlearning continues.

Out of the corner of my eye, I see Reframing scuttle under dismantled floorboards.

"You loved your father Calvin. You loved him as much as you possibly could. You didn't replace him with Percy. *You are allowed to love them both.*"

"I should've tried harder," Should's words come out of my mouth. "I didn't do enough. It was so much easier to just do what Mom and Percy said, to stop fighting them about Calvin. What kind of person does that make me? Keating didn't deserve it. How could I have been so stupid and so blind for all those years? How could I still care about someone who taught Keating that who he was, who he loved, was bad? How could Keating *ever* love anyone when he didn't love himself? Especially when the person that he wants to love reflects what he's been taught to hate? How can I even care about people that not just believe that kind of bigotry, but teach it to children?"

I curl into myself and sob incoherently.

Unlearning shocks me by mirroring my position. I don't even hear Reframing anymore, but I know he's busy. I know he's knocking things down because I feel it. There are so many walls in me; so many I didn't build, so many I hid behind.

I show Unlearning all my Shame; all the beliefs I accepted at Should's insistence. I'm too fat. I'm not ever going to be smart enough. I don't deserve my husband. I could've changed everything if only I had stood up for Keating. He would have accepted himself and loved himself. He wouldn't have become an addict. He wouldn't have killed himself. If I had taken care of Charles like I was supposed to, he would still be here, too. He was *my* responsibility. By leaving the hospital when my mom asked me to stay, she died lonely and sad.

I don't deserve good things in my life. I'm not allowed to enjoy the things I worked hard for. If I don't put others first, they won't love me.

My beliefs don't always make sense, but Unlearning listens. She says the words I need to hear to combat them. She tells me that these beliefs don't belong to me. Not really. They belong to Percy, to Kate, even Keating. They belong to that boy that I dated who told me that I looked whorish in red and hurt me when the number on the scale wasn't to his liking. She tells me over and over again that these beliefs aren't mine. They sound like me because the people who installed those beliefs, that faulty foundation - they know me. They laid that foundation with the help of a child's innocent trust; a child who didn't know better.

"But now that you do know better," Unlearning reminds me. "It's up to us to rip everything out and start from the ground up. It's a lot of work, but it's important. If we don't do it, you will perpetuate exactly what you're trying to heal from."

Reframing knocks down walls and rips up the floorboards. Together we build a new foundation. One that looks like me. One that I choose.

They don't rush me. We take breaks when I'm exhausted. Taggart is there. He doesn't rush me, either. He hugs me. He takes me on dates. He makes me laugh. He listens. He encourages me to reach out to my friends; the ones that really see me the way he does. They all know this renovation has been a long time coming. They're happy I'm finally doing it.

Taggart tells me that he's proud of me. He tells me he sees what I'm doing, and he knows it's hard. He says he wishes he could do it for me, but he knows I have to do this on my own.

After a couple of years of hearing his support and encouragement, I begin allowing myself to feel it. The more I accept it, the more I feel it, the more my brand-new foundation stabilizes.

"There's something else over here," Reframing says, forehead drenched with sweat.

Dazed, I climb to my feet, and on shaking legs walk across debris to a huge wall. It takes up so much space that I can't believe I've never seen it before.

"What is that?"

I'm unsure where it ends and where it begins.

Reframing yanks a bandana out of his back pocket, mopping up his face.

"That's Grief, kid."

I feel the deep abyss of emptiness in me. "I thought Grief was, you know. A feeling."

"He is." Unlearning says. "All the walls we knocked down to create space? Those were feelings that became so real they became walls. That numbness in you that didn't let you receive Love? That was the foundation you stood on. Grief is a bit different."

Iris grasps my hand tightly. She knows I need her for this.

Reframing looks at me with pity in his eyes. "Listen, kid. This is a bit more recent, and it's not yet gotten to the foundation, but it can creep into other areas. It takes a long time, so we'll stick around, but that doesn't mean you aren't doing your part. We need to know what we're working with, and we need to start now. Otherwise, it's going to encroach into your nice new foundation. If that happens then all that work, we just went through will be shot to hell."

"Okay." My voice is small.

Should wants me to be scared. I'm not. Her face doesn't look quite so perfect anymore, but it doesn't matter. That's not what I'm looking at.

"Lay it on me, Reframing," I say. "I trust you."

He takes off his work gloves and places his calloused hands on the brick wall.

"This is Grief, right?"

"Yes."

"Grief is always here. He can show up at any time, for any reason."

"Okay."

Unlearning and Iris are holding hands, too. I've never seen that before, but something about it makes me feel lighter inside.

Reframing is talking to me. He tells me that Grief is different for every relationship; that I'm allowed to feel it more sharply for some than for others. That sometimes it's more real when I don't expect it to be, and that there might be days where I don't feel it at all.

"But if I don't feel it, then that means I'm moving on without them. It means that I've accepted they're not here."

I sense Fear and Shame lurking, but instead of keeping them quiet, I hear my own admission. "Shame and Fear show up a lot with Grief."

I'm staring at the wall, transfixed. It ripples under Reframing's hands.

"With Calvin, I mourn the father I could have had rather than him as a person. I feel so bad about that, especially after everything he missed out on. I do remember more about him now than I did in the past..."

My voice trails off and Reframing says, "That's trauma. You were real young, and when we dismantled the old foundation, we reworked that part of you that shut the Love for him down. You weren't allowed to love him."

He pauses here before gently asking, "What happened if you did?"

My mind flashes back to Keating being spanked for calling Calvin 'Dad'.

"We were punished."

"Right," Reframing places another dried lavender bit in his mouth to chew on. "Your Love for him was real complicated. Because of that, so is your Grief."

I nod in understanding.

Now Reframing goes on to tell me more about Keating.

"Keating is real complicated for you. Percy liked you better –"

Iris urges me to interject with, "Percy could control me more."

Reframing smiles at Unlearning as he continues. "Exactly. That's not your fault either. To take advantage of a child's Love, of a child's desire for her father. That has nothing to do with you. You loved the father you were allowed to love. You loved the father you were given. And that's it, kid. Because you saw how he was with Keating, how he was with your mom, you think you aren't still allowed to care? You are. It's complicated to love the people who hurt you. It's complicated to love the people who made you watch while they hurt the people *you* love. That doesn't mean you aren't allowed to feel how you feel. You can be angry and hurt by it, but still love them. Remember - they installed your old foundation. They manipulated you, kid. You loved the family you were given with everything you had. That doesn't mean it's simple or comfortable, and because of that neither is your Grief."

I lose track of how long Reframing has to repeat this. Unlearning and Iris are embracing one another as I shift the thoughts in my mind like a game of emotional Tetris.

They know that for me Percy and Keating are intertwined. They know that there have been many times that Keating acted just like Percy; hurting me, physically, emotionally. As I think about this, as I sit with it, I realize that Keating lashed out at me because he knew that I would always be there for him. Even when he tried to kill himself, though we weren't talking because I had asked Loss to come take our relationship until he could treat me with respect, Keating knew I would show up to take care of him.

"He knew I loved him." The words fall out of my mouth. "He knew I'd take care of him when it mattered. Because I did." I pause here for a moment. "I took care of him the best way I could."

Reframing claps, just once as the wall starts to ripple even more. I'm not looking at it, but I hear him yell. "That's it, kid!"

Reframing talks to me about my mom, about how I was a combination of friend, rival, and daughter and how it was very confusing.

"She'd punish you for what you wrote in your journal one minute and then be your best friend the next. Kate loved you, no doubt, but she let Percy demean you. She even started to participate in it. She was two different people, so of course, how you feel about her is complicated. You loved her so much, but she didn't have friends. Her world was very small. She was jealous of your friendships and freedoms, yet she wanted more for you. She had blinders on, and there were glimpses when you saw her, the real her."

There are memories of Mom flooding me now, complex, painful, and reassuring all the same.

Reframing goes on about Charles, about how my Grief for him is both as sister and parent, because that's the role I had with him.

"Kate knew you'd take care of him. That's on her and adds layers of even more complication for both you and her, and you and Charles. Loss came for Charles' childhood, and you gave yours to spare his."

I cry at this, like I always do. Charles is always hard for me. Reframing and I spend a lot of time on Charles. Shame is strong here and fighting him is painful.

"It's all so complicated," I tell Reframing. "It's so muddy. There are times when it's so sharp I feel like I could die from the pain of it, but then. Then there are times when it's so comforting." I pause here, unpacking it with Iris as she nudges me to speak my truth.

"It's comforting because it's what I know. There was such kindness in Charles. Such light. I couldn't bear to watch it go out."

Unlearning comes to me now, holding my face between her cool hands. "Grief is never just one thing, Emerson. It's a million things. And how we love is often how we grieve. Because of the complexities, because of the muddiness, your grief is not clear. Your grief is a reflection of your relationship; each individual relationship, as well as the family dynamic."

We sit like that for a while, me accepting that Grief will never look how I want it to. That Grief will never be what I expect. And that Grief will be a mirror, not only of my relationship with them but of the Love that was both given and received. It finally dawns on me, what this wall is. What Grief is.

I flash back to when Grief showed up and showed me the contracts that I had signed in Love.

"Grief is Love." The words spill from my mouth, and with a mixture of exhaustion and enlightenment, I continue.

"Love is complicated. So, Grief is complicated. It makes sense. They're the same. Grief is what happens with the Love for someone or something, that no longer exists. But here — in my mind, in my memories, in my soul — they'll always exist. They're imprinted on me and in me; in my foundation, in my walls, in the very fabric that makes up who I am. I can't tear down this wall, can I?"

I look up to see Reframing, Unlearning, and Iris shaking their heads at me.

"No," Iris tells me. "You can't."

"I don't really want to though, do I?" I pose the question more to myself than I do to them. And in realizing I don't want to take it down; I alone hold the power over what I want it to be.

I'm the architect of my mind, after all. So, if I need this wall, if it's structural, what can I do with it?

I place my hands on the wall that is both Love and Grief and let them both fill me. Memories of when they were alive. Memories of when they weren't. And I know.

What was once an impassable brick wall, has become a beautiful archway. There are still bricks; places in the wall I can't get through; but in the center, are stunning windowed doors reaching to the ceiling. They let light in. If I open them, they let Love in, too.

Unconditional Love

*One is loved because one is loved. No reason
is needed for loving.* – Paulo Coelho

I eye the Love streaming in warily. I want it. I really do. I just don't
know what I have to do to deserve it.

"Okay, so if Grief is Love," I begin reciting my newfound
knowledge like a child memorizing a flashcard. "And Fear is the
other side of Love, then doesn't it stand to reason that Fear is coming
through those doors, too?"

Cautious, I step around the Love I see pouring in. It's beautiful, It
really is. I want it so badly, but I'm distracted by the files that are in its
path. I know now that I'm allowed to love Percy. I'm allowed to love
Calvin. But reconciling how I feel about people who are gone, doesn't
change the fact that Fear is still here. Creating piles. Terrifying me.

"I know that Taggart loves me. I know that," I promise Unlearning
and Reframing. "I know that the more work I do on myself, the more
I improve, the better a person I become the more he loves me."

I wait for Iris to solidify this knowing, but she doesn't.

Unlearning steps forward, brow furrowed. "What do you mean,
the more work you do and the more you improve?"

I explain to her that I understand that Grief is Love. I explain to her that I understand that Taggart loves me, that my friends love me. I understand that I'm allowed to feel it and put my needs first, because when I take care of myself that's how I earn their Love.

Iris sweeps in next to Unlearning. Reframing crouches down next to me. I don't realize it, but I'm in a river of Fear's files. I'm surrounded by logic, by reason, by something that makes so much sense to me.

Fear stretches their arms and says, "Nice try guys. Maybe you'll get her next time."

But Unlearning is having none of this. She sits on the ground next to me.

"Oh, don't." I urge her to stand up. "You'll get that gorgeous suit all dirty."

She brushes off my words like she brushes the dust from her pants. "I don't care about my suit, Emerson. I care about you."

We're all in Fear, now. Only Iris is above us. She won't stoop to Fear's level. I know it.

Though they are entrenched in Fear with me, they do not succumb as I do. Reframing is quiet as Unlearning continues to ask about the link between Fear and Love.

"I've never loved someone and not been afraid they would leave." Of my own volition, I play them the scenes from Shame's reel, and the scenes from Fear's inception. "I came across these again with Meditation, back when I initially planted Iris, to help."

"That isn't all you planted," Meditation appears next to Iris.

"I didn't know who else to call," Reframing says almost apologetically.

Meditation pulls me out of Fear, and into the space where it is just her and Iris and me. I try to fight. I don't want to leave Reframing and Unlearning alone. Fear is contagious.

"Meditation can we bring them with us? They've done so much for me…I owe them…" gnawing on my lip, I glance over my shoulder waiting for Fear to appear.

"Emerson," Iris swaddles me like a child. "Breathe."

She and Mediation take me through my steps.

Breathe in fresh air.
Breathe out negative thoughts.

Back in my mind with my selves, I feel centered. Except now it's not a past self, it's a future self. And she's sitting right in front of me.

Future Me holds out her hands for mine, and I grasp them. Mine are a bit shaky, and hers are steady. Warm. Reassuring.

"I'm so sorry," I apologize to her before I can help it. Tears are leaking from my eyes, but I don't know why.

She slowly recedes. Once again, I am alone with Iris and Mediation.

"Why did you feel compelled to apologize to her?" Meditation asks me this question. I don't have a clear answer.

Iris reverberates in every molecule of my energy, and I hear myself say, "I don't know what I'm missing. I know I'm missing something to move forward. I need more than Unlearning and Reframing."

"Mmmm." Iris responds.

I'm taken back to my mind, and though I am confused by the visit with Meditation, I'm confident in the direction we're heading. I have faith in Iris, and in having faith in Iris, I have faith in myself.

"I won't apologize for leaving," I tell Reframing and Unlearning who are right where I left them. "I know that you've come here to help and do a great deal of work with me, but as you taught me, I needed to put myself first. Fear overtakes me sometimes, in the form of crippling confusion or slippery logic. I know that I left you alone with Fear, but I needed some time to regroup."

Iris hugs me, and I feel her pride.

"Our work isn't done, is it?"

"No, Emerson," Iris says. "If you still believe you have to earn someone's Love, if you still believe that you can lose it as well, then our work is far from finished."

I reach down to help Reframing and Unlearning up from the ground.

"You didn't leave us alone for no reason," Reframing says, a box of files in his hands. "We did some research. Unlearning is hell on research."

She smiles at the compliment and thanks Reframing.

"That's true. I do love my research. true. I do love my research. I must tell you; we've learned quite a bit. So, we're not finished, if you'll still have us."

Despite the baggage of Fear trailing me, I laugh. "Yes, I will."

We find a corner of my mind to let Unlearning read quietly and leave her to it. Reframing and I walk around the newly renovated space. He's got a broom and a dustpan, sweeping away any remnants of belief that aren't mine.

"She has to learn what you learn. We've rebuilt the foundation, we've taken down walls, now it's time for her to figure out what's in those files Fear has been collecting over the years. There's a heck of a lot of them," he adds with a shake of his head. "We got rid of some of them when we did the remodel. Some new foundation boards, took down some walls that you thought were structural but were just calcified Fear files."

Surprised, I say, "I didn't know Fear could become calcified and turn into a wall?"

"Happens all the time," Reframing responds. "We're not a one and done sort of renovation. We handle the upkeep too."

"I didn't know that. How much does that cost?" I try to remember the number he showed me. I can't remember much time and effort he said it would be. It has to be a lot more than I realized.

He waves his hand dismissively. "It was all included in the price I gave you. We come back when we're needed. And now that you're familiar with our work, it'll be much more comfortable for you to know when you need us. Hopefully it won't always be so intense or take so long, especially with the new foundation. We know a renovation takes a lot out of you."

I hug him. I can't help it. He's so sweet and considerate, and though he looks like a gruff little Santa Claus, he's so strong and helpful.

"Thank you," I effusively repeat. "Thank you. Thank you."

Iris fills me with the understanding that these new friends of mine, Reframing, and his dear colleague Unlearning, hardworking and intense though they may be, only want the things that I want. That they will help me be the best version of myself.

As this dawning washes over me, Unlearning clips over in her heels. She's brisk, to the point, but there's an underlying tone of tenderness in her voice.

"I've read some of these files, and they're pretty self-explanatory."

I reach for one. "Oh? Let me see."

Unlearning pulls it closer to her chest. "No. It's safer for me to read Fear's files than it is for you."

"It is?"

I try to shrug off the feeling of Iris yanking me back from the file, but I stop myself. I remind myself that Iris is here to help me. I remind myself that they all are.

"Yes," Unlearning starts. "For me to do what I do, to help you Unlearn something that is detrimental to you, for Reframing to help you shift that perspective, we first have to know what we're dealing with. We inspected your foundation, your walls, your ceiling. Now, we inspect the information that it has held, and in doing so we are able to understand it. To get rid of your Fear, you first must understand it."

As I listen to her prattle on about the importance of understanding Fear in order to evict it, I am reminded of Dr. Q. The affection in Unlearning's tone, the care Reframing took when considering the time and cost, they both remind me of that moment when Dr. Q said he cared about me. He was doing a job - a job to help me. But he didn't *have* to care. That's what made me uncomfortable. That's what made me so angry. I didn't understand where it had come from. I paid him for a job, that's true. But you can't pay someone to love you.

"Love." I say interrupting their powwow. "It has to do with Love."

Iris looks over at Reframing and Unlearning. "It's as I told you," she tells them. "We need her."

"Who?" I ask, bewildered.

"Unconditional Love."

Reframing and Unlearning leave. It's me and Iris, and the Others, though they're not nearly as unruly. They're still around, still doing their jobs, but it feels softer. Less. Like a massive diffuser has been put on their microphones and I can only hear their muffled attempts. When Shame tries to show me a reel, I get pulled in, but sometimes I can quickly pull myself out. And other times, I can simply say "No thanks, mate. Not today."

On those days he stalks off, furious. I don't care where he goes as long as it's not here.

Iris and I wait for Unconditional Love, but to be honest, I'm nervous about it. I'm familiar with her, although there's never a time in my life when I've encountered her where she hasn't made me uncomfortable.

"I know," Iris says to me when I mention this to her. She pours some of her soothing calm over the troubled water that is my Fear and tells me to trust her. I have no choice. She hasn't steered me wrong yet. I know that she won't.

It begins a day like any other, which is to say unlike any other. I'm doing better. I'm taking my Prozac. I'm showering when I first wake up in the morning - mostly. I'm putting clothes on and creating some semblance of a routine. Taggart and I live in New York now. I've wanted to live here for as long as I can remember. It turned out that Taggart had also. We spent so much time and effort working toward this one goal: To move here. To live here. To stay here.

And we do. We have a wonderful apartment. We have two dogs. We have each other. I wake up next to my best friend and look out my window to the most beautiful view I've ever seen. I can't believe I live here. I can't believe Taggart wants to. I can't believe this is my life.

And before I register it, Fear comes in.

Fear tells me that Taggart is the one who has made the financial choices for us to live here, and I've done nothing to earn it. Fear tells me that I had better enjoy this while I can, because it won't last.

Living in New York is the first dream that has come true for me. It's the only thing that I've always wanted. From the first time I'd seen it in a movie, to the first time I read about it in a book, to the first moment I physically stepped onto Manhattan, I knew this is where I was meant to be. So when Taggart and I are finally living here after nearly ten years of hard work, dedication, and sacrifice, I am terrified.

"I'm so used to waiting for the other shoe to drop," I tell Iris as we walk in the park on a cool, crisp day. "It feels strange when it doesn't. Then I just end up dropping it myself."

There, in the middle of my favorite place in the world, with the light shining down through the verdant leaves, Unconditional Love drops in.

"Why must we drop it?"

She is – in a word – breathtaking. I want to compare her beauty to Iris, but I can't. It's the same, yet different. She is luminously, incredibly real. I feel her. I recognize her. She is the Love I can't understand. She is the Love that makes me uncomfortable. She is the Love I don't have to earn.

"Of course, you don't have to earn me." The words flow from her like water in a stream. "No one has to earn me. I simply am."

She looks into my eyes, her elegant fingers under my chin. "I make you uncomfortable."

"Yes." And shy, but I don't say that out loud.

She makes a noncommittal sound. We sit in awkward silence, made even more awkward by the fact that I don't know what to say. And though Iris is all around us, she too, is silent.

"You know," Unconditional Love begins, and her voice reminds me so much of floating. Or flying. It brings to mind a warm velvet breeze washing over me in all its silky splendor. The dulcet tones of Charles' laughter. The sharp triumph of Keating's joyous cackle. I am lost in memories of building forts with my brothers, laughing with my mother, and the sight of Calvin's face when he first saw me in the Tucson airport.

"Ah, a wonderful place to start." Unconditional Love gestures to all that is around me. The melodic saxophone warbling a few benches away, like the background of a Nora Ephron movie. The hopeful buds of flowers yet to bloom. The peace in knowing that I don't have to rush this visit, because I live here.

"You deserve to be here," she tells me. The lack of inflection in her voice, the matter-of-fact way it is delivered only makes it more impactful.

"I do?"

"You do. You worry that Taggart won't be happy here. You worry that he moved here because you wanted it so desperately. Because this is the place you feel at home. It isn't why. Taggart loves it as well. It's unfathomable to you that you could have a man who shares not only your bed but your dreams, but you can. You do."

I start to spin out. "It doesn't feel real. I just … I don't know what I did to deserve this."

Urgent now, she takes me by the shoulders. "Nothing. And everything."

I'm confused and annoyed. "I hate how you all talk in such riddles."

Iris joins in and we all laugh at this.

"She's right you know," Iris points out.

Unconditional Love nods in assent. "Let me speak plainly then."

We are still in the park. I gaze up at the trees in my favorite section of The Mall with Unconditional Love taking over my entire consciousness. There is no room for anything but her and Iris, and the view I have before me.

"I spoke with Unlearning." Unconditional Love tells me. "She has allowed me to speak in her stead. This is something that requires a great bit of focus on your part, I'm afraid. And I believe it's best done in the place you feel most yourself, most at home, most unencumbered. With as few cooks in the kitchen, let's say, as possible."

I nod my head in understanding. "I respect that."

Iris fuses herself to me in every possible way. I know that what is transpiring is not only necessary to heal from the past, but essential in order to move forward.

"You have been taught from a very young age, that you must earn Love. No, please don't interrupt," Unconditional Love gently admonishes me when I make a move to object. "I know that when good things happen to you, you're afraid to enjoy them. You're afraid to allow yourself the joy that accompanies them. This is Fear's power over you. It was planted in you by the very people who were meant to plant me instead."

She stares off into the sky now, and I follow her gaze. Two birds dance in the sunlight and we watch for a bit as this information sinks in.

"The abuse you were forced to witness – Keating's beatings, the name calling, the withholding of care and affection – that level of manipulation and Fear in the name of Love, was as bad as what was done to Keating."

She lets me sit with this for a while, and I do. I want to interrupt her to tell her that's not true, that Keating had it worse, but filled top to bottom, inside and out with Iris, I know that isn't true.

"I'm not a victim." I say defiantly.

"You were." Unconditional Love holds my face in hers. "You didn't stay a victim, but you were. This, you need to accept."

"I don't want to." Fat tears roll down my cheeks. Exasperated with myself, I can't help but complain. "This is ridiculous. Am I ever not crying?"

"It's wonderful that you're finally feeling your emotions, Emerson. I'm proud of you."

When she tells me this, my vision blurs even more, and no amount of blinking will clear it.

Unconditional Love tells me that my Love has been used against me. "You've been taught to think that if you help people, if you save them; if when you are feeling your lowest, you reach out to check on someone else, you will be loved."

I don't need to confirm this. She knows.

"There is a difference between kindness and feeling like you have to earn someone's Love. Your kindness, your Love, has been used against you."

She plays the scene now where my first memory of Fear began. With new perspective, I watch.

"You weren't physically hurt, Emerson. But you *were* hurt."

I feel the dull raking in my stomach that means I'm going to hear something I don't want to hear. I reach out blindly searching for Iris, remembering at the last moment to reach inside for her, not out.

"They knew what they were doing," Unconditional Love explains. "They knew it would be more painful for you to watch someone you love be hurt than for you to be hurt. They knew you were the key."

"The key to what?"

"The key to their manipulations. You love them so deeply still. You, Emerson, were the perfect example of what I am. You were the perfect example of Unconditional Love. All you wanted was for everyone to be happy, to form a unit. So, they formed a unit and left Keating out. Soon, even you left Keating out because you trusted them. You were allowed to trust them. How could you know?"

Should joins us on the bench. "You should've known better. What kind of person thinks that's normal?"

Unconditional Love reaches out and, with a featherlight touch, caresses my face. "A child. A child who didn't know any better. A child who trusted the people who took care of her."

This hurts. I want Unconditional Love to judge me. I want her to tell me I could've stopped it. That's more comfortable than this support, this light that surrounds her. I don't know how to respond to this.

"No, you've never known how to respond to receiving it. Yet, you always give it."

I hate that I understand what she means. And there, in the middle of Central Park, like the New Yorker I've always longed to be, I break down.

"I'm familiar with you from Charles. He just loved everyone no matter what. He was so kind. He was so young. I miss him so much."

Wiping my eyes, I laugh to myself. "He heard this quote from a movie and though it was said in a really funny way, he used to say it seriously all the time. 'Everybody love everybody.'"

Unconditional Love embraces me, embraces the memory of Charles. "Yes. Charles had the right of it."

We leave it here, and I walk the long way home. Over the next few weeks, I think about what Unconditional Love shared with me. How my mom and Percy knew what they were doing. How my Love was used against me as a manipulation tactic.

"It explains a lot," I admit to Iris. "It explains why I've found many friendships and relationships where I am the giver, and they are the taker. I find comfort in that. It explains why when I first met Frankie, I tried to push her away and cling tighter at the same time. It explains why even now when Grief or Depression show up, I retreat and handle it myself, not letting anyone in to help. It explains why when Shame and Should show up, especially if they're not mine, I get defensive."

"You're starting to see," Iris responds.

"What? What am I starting to see?"

Iris' gaze shines on me, and I see the Unconditional Love in it. "That you don't have to be afraid."

I don't want to be afraid of Unconditional Love. She's beautiful and bright, and surprisingly bold. She's easy to be with once I get past my inherent discomfort. And I really want to get past it.

"No, you don't. If you get comfortable with her, if you get used to her, what are you going to do when she's not around anymore?"

Fear has shown up, asking their questions yet again. Except this time, I knew it was coming. And this time, I have a question for them.

"Where is she going to go?"

Fear balks at the audacity of my accusatory tone. "Where?! ANYWHERE!"

I feel how frantic they are, but somehow the more frantic Fear feels regarding Unconditional Love, the more at ease I feel about her.

"I know you don't show up on your own," I tell Fear. "I know someone planted you in my mind, the same way I planted the light of Intuition. I know you're scared of Unconditional Love."

"That's ridiculous," Fear says, but they scamper off when I feel Unconditional Love come in.

"Hello, Emerson." She hugs me, and instinctively I hug her

back. She feels so real. More solid than Shame. More tangible than Depression. She feels like the wall that Grief was, and all at once I know she is. I know she is more real, more solid than all of them together. I have only to believe. I have only to accept.

"I want you to be with me," I say to her shyly. "As often as possible. How do we – how do I – do that?"

She smiles radiantly. Her smile – her spirit – is so brilliant that it illuminates my entire being, eviscerating any darkness that remains lurking in the corners of my mind.

"You can't just be comfortable with me. We must make it so that I am stronger and more plentiful than Fear, and in doing that we have to accept things. Good things. I know you're used to putting everyone first, and I know that Unlearning and Reframing helped you understand that you come first. That is a huge step."

There's a moment of hesitation here.

"When you are raised with Conditional Love rather than the Unconditional Love a child is meant to be raised with, it feels quite conflicting to you. You spend your life trying to figure out how to come to terms with it, how to not be terrified of Love and Joy. It feels somehow factual and logical, in the least emotional of ways and that is Fear's root. We must yank it out."

Transfixed, I ask, "How?"

Together she and Iris hold my hands. "By understanding that all Love that is not Unconditional Love is logic and manipulation. You were taught that if you don't do something well enough, you don't deserve the Love. It was dangled in front of you like a carrot in front of a horse. The lie you were fed is that it's just waiting for you. And if only you had done this better, then you would have it."

As she says this, I hear my mom's voice telling me that Calvin didn't want to see me anymore. I see Percy crouched in front of me telling me he loves me after Keating has been punished for calling Calvin Dad. I see the boy who claimed to love me while turning my skin black and blue. I see myself looking in my own mirror picking apart my body for its flaws first. I hear Fear telling me that Taggart will die. Or leave. I hear Fear tell me that I will be all alone, and that it will be my own fault. I feel the comfort of Fear, that sweater I have worn for years. Perfectly washed. Perfectly worn in.

"I feel more comfortable wrapped in Fear, in Depression, in Grief than I do with you." I hear myself saying.

"I know," Unconditional Love says.

Deliberately I swathe myself in Iris. "It's too easy to get lost in the 'am I enough? Am I loving enough? Am I giving this person everything that this person needs? Am I reflecting the love that they've given me?' I'm already planning for the day that I will have to live without Taggart, without the ones I love, without myself. That's no way to live - because in that way, in that sense, I guess I'm already living without them."

"Yes," Iris encourages me. "Yes."

Scrubbing my face with my hands, I continue. "I've spent my entire life trying to control everything, trying to prepare for all contingencies. And all it's taught me; all Fear has taught me is how to manipulate other people."

I let out a huge sigh and feel the sweater of Fear get tighter and tighter. It's not getting smaller. I'm just outgrowing it.

"I don't *want* to manipulate other people. I don't want to be a toxic person. I know I have to have been toxic to some people if I let Fear in to manipulate others in the name of Love. I don't want to do that anymore. I don't want to have this false armor up anymore, Iris. I just want to be myself. My true, authentic self. And I want to love myself. How do I do that?"

Unconditional Love joins Iris, wrapping herself around me as she answers my question.

"By understanding that any Love that is weaponized in *any* capacity is not truly Love. Love is not a weapon. It is not to be wielded, at yourself or anyone else, like a medieval sword in the name of protection. It is something to be given and received with no agenda. No demands. Only wishing to exist. Therefore, it is my belief the only actual Love, is Unconditional Love."

I am swaddled in Unconditional Love and Intuition. I feel safe. I feel whole. I get it. I finally get it. No Love is greater or less than another. It simply is. And to deprive myself of that Love is to deprive the ones I love as well. And somehow, miraculously, I know that just because I didn't receive it as a child, doesn't mean it's too late to receive it now.

"I need to love myself the way I love others; wholly, without reserve or judgement."

I see the light pouring in through the doors of Grief. The boxes of files that belong to Fear are gone. I look around for Unconditional Love, and it hits me. Unconditional Love; the truest, purest, most authentic Love. The only kind of Love. Unconditional Love is Love. Love is all that matters. It is as simple and as complicated as that.

Stepping toward Grief, I yank the doors open. I let Love shine on absolutely everything. Especially me. Arms flung out, I spin around laughing and laughing until I become so dizzy from joy that I nearly topple over. Grief is holding hands with Love, and with full understanding, I embrace them both.

"I don't need to do anything to deserve Love. I never have."

And, with Iris inside me shining like a beacon, I believe it.

Boundaries

The more you value yourself, the healthier your boundaries are.
– Lorraine Nilon

I feel good. Raw. Exposed. But good. It's been a long time since I've felt this good. I don't know if I ever have. I feel like I'm discovering who I am. Who I want to be. I'm allowed to ask myself what I need and put myself first. I'm allowed to feel the full meaning behind Taggart's 'I love you's'. I'm allowed to love myself. And I do.

Grief's pain is much less acute. He feels like a bruise that I've long since acclimated to; the kind that I forget about because I'm so accustomed to the dull throbbing. Though sometimes when I least expect it, I run into something that hits the bruise that Grief has become. When this happens, it hurts like the first time; its pain echoing through me, hulling me out. It shocks me all over again since I'm no longer acclimated to the sharp vacuity of his torment.

But it's okay. I've been training for this. Each time it happens, I rebound faster even if I don't know the cause. Mostly, he's just there, hanging out in the background. And wherever he is, Love is always close by.

The life I'm living now is so different than it was when Loss and

Death took my family, that it's hard to imagine them here. I don't live in the same town or the same apartment, so I don't feel haunted by where I was when I got Loss's calls. I don't feel like an interloper in Taggart's family anymore. I text my sisters-in-law. I know my nieces' individual styles and look forward to buying them presents. I know which nephew likes skyscrapers and which nephew prefers nunchucks.

I still think about my family's holiday traditions. I still wonder.

What would Charles look like? Would my mom like the way I've decorated my apartment? Would Keating and Taggart be friends? Would Calvin have visited me here? Would Percy?

Wondering about them, missing them, has become its own tradition. One I'm accustomed to and never get used to in equal measure. It's a tradition that doesn't wait for the holidays, even though I don't cry when we drive by Percy's exit anymore.

There are days when I don't think about any of them at all. When this happens, Shame shows up and I can't shake him. I don't want to pay him any attention, but he's implacable.

"How can you just go on about your life like they're not here?"

"Because they're not, Shame."

I tell him this every time. I try to explain that Grief and Love are partners; two sides of the same coin. I try to explain to him that Love is a part of everything and because I don't stop loving them, that means *they* are a part of everything. I try to explain to him that Love and Grief are intrinsically linked, and that I have found a way to exist in the aftermath of Loss, without letting myself drown in her. I try to explain to him that I can't let Grief take over every aspect of my life – that while Grief is with me forever, I am working really, really hard to have a life of my own. A happy one.

"I don't want to spiral. I don't want new input. I don't want you to come around anymore," sternly admonishing him, I do my best to sound authoritative.

We fight about this, and I don't know how to stop him. He seems to slither into even the tiniest of openings. He's upset that my new foundation has so drastically altered his. His attempts to draw me into the shadowed corners of my own mind are relentless. Shame is a creature of darkness, after all. He's never done well in the light.

"I need to really do something about him," I tell Iris.

She is steadily reassuring as ever. "Yes, you do."

"How?" This boggles me. Shame is canny. He's even started to shift a bit, and he's brought Should in on his transformation. They tell me they're just looking out for me.

"You already know."

I call Love in. She's always around me, inside me. She doesn't judge me. She doesn't judge anyone, and honestly, she's kind of astonishing.

"Love, I need some help."

She sits with me on the floor in my living room, meeting me at my level.

"If I can help, I will."

Iris and I share a sweet smile. Love is a fixer of worlds, yet she is so very humble.

I explain to her about Shame. I tell her that he's still sneaking in, still adapting. He's hanging out in the corner of my mind feeding on some of Fear's old files; the ones that aren't detrimental to my mental health. Yet.

"Ah, I see." She nods her head, understanding where I'm coming from. "What would you like to do?"

"Ideally I'd like to get rid of him altogether. Is that even possible?"

"There is something we can do. Someone we can call. He's very good at this sort of thing." Love taps her fingers to her lips. "Iris?"

Iris is already nodding. "Yes. I think it's time."

"Who is he?"

"Boundaries," Love responds.

I'm shocked. "I didn't think Boundaries and Love went together?"

Laughing she waves her hand. "That's a very common misconception. Boundaries is one of my dearest, dearest friends. He's another of my forms."

"Wait. So, you're saying that Boundaries is another form of Love?"

Iris gleams with knowing. I am deeply surprised at this. I always thought that Boundaries were bad, especially when it came to Love.

"You're confusing 'boundaries' with 'limits'," Iris corrects me.

"Aren't they the same thing?"

"Not when it comes to Love. *Limiting* how much Love you have, or give, refers to capacity – how much you want to share, how much you're willing to allow yourself to receive. You've done this before," Love recalls. "When you thought I was something to be earned or lost."

"Okay, I follow what you're saying. Though, I'm still a little confused."

Iris fills me with understanding, while Love walks to the door.

"I called in reinforcements," she says smiling.

Unlearning and Reframing stride in, and both sit next to me, cross legged on the ground. I am full of Love at this. They are all so willing to consistently meet me at my level.

"Think of it like this, kid." Reframing starts, chewing his signature stalk of dried lavender. "You and Frankie have been friends for a long time, right?"

"Yes."

"In fact, you've known Frankie longer than you've known Taggart, right?"

"Yes," I answer tentatively.

"Would you show up to her house without calling and just let yourself in?"

I guffaw so loudly I surprise myself. "There are multiple things wrong with that sentence."

Everyone looks at each other, then at me.

"Enlighten us," Unlearning replies. "Please."

"Well, first of all, I would never just show up to her house unannounced," I counter. "It doesn't matter how long we've known each other. To begin with, she has kids. They could be napping. They could be having friends over. She could be working. Her husband could be working from home. She could be needing a day to herself, and I would interrupt that time. I don't know their schedule.

Furthermore, it's not their job to tell me their schedule. There are a million factors here. And I would absolutely not just let myself into her house. For all the reasons I just mentioned and oh about a thousand more."

"Whynot?" Love asks me.

"Out of respect. It doesn't matter how long we've known each other – I know her. She would hate that. Now Meg for example?" I mention, thinking of how some of my other friends would respond to this. "I couldn't just show up there unannounced, but most of the time I do just let myself in. Darcy? Darcy would be fine with me showing up without calling, and honestly would probably be fine with me letting myself in, too. I don't know if I would do that because of her dogs, but still."

I stop talking, completely bemused as to why everyone is staring at me with such self-satisfied looks on their faces.

"What?"

Reframing brightens merrily. "You hit the nail on the head. Respect. You respect them, right?"

I fight the urge to roll my eyes. "Of course I do."

Unlearning leans in toward me, laying her hand over mine. "Does this make you love them any less?"

I laugh again. "Of course not. Why would it?"

She ignores my question and before I can ask again, she holds up a finger. "And you know that Frankie's needs and response would be very different than that of Meg or Darcy?"

I'm starting to get annoyed. "Yes, of course."

"How do you know?" Love leans in now, linking arms with me.

"Because they've told me."

"Exactly!" Love kisses me on the cheek and, though I'm still annoyed, I laugh at her exuberance.

"Could you please explain it to me – and not spoon-feed it to me like I'm a five-year-old?"

They all look to Unlearning. She nods in silent understanding that this is hers to explain.

"You love these women, deeply. They've become your family - your tribe. Yet, they all need different things, and you don't hesitate for a minute about respecting that fact; respecting their very different and very separate needs."

"No," I say slowly unsure where she's going with this. "They're all different people. Different people have different needs."

"Exactly," she repeats, jabbing a finger in the air for emphasis. "What would happen if you did just let yourself into Frankie's home unannounced?"

"I would never do that." My response is automatic.

"Because …" she leads.

"Because that's crossing a line for her. I value our friendship and her needs, too much to cross a line."

Unlearning high-fives me, and it's so out of character for her that I scrunch my face in delight.

"Emerson," she starts to tell me, pulling Love to her feet. "That's a boundary. You love Frankie, and by respecting a boundary that she has you continue to love her. Not only that, but you also make her feel even more loved for respecting it. Does her having that boundary limit how much you love her?"

"Why would it?"

I see where she's going with this. Boundaries are another form of respect. I wouldn't ever intentionally cross a boundary that someone has laid before me. I wouldn't ever ask someone to neglect their own Boundaries for me.

"So, what does this have to do with Shame? It feels like we've gotten a little off track."

Unlearning takes her leave, having done what she came to do. And Reframing hops up, eager to get to work.

"Shame doesn't like Boundaries. He doesn't have any, so he doesn't respect them. But uh," Reframing sheepishly scratches the back of neck. "Boundaries is really strong and it's – as Love said – another of her forms. That means that Boundaries has the power of Love behind him and that's pretty much what we're all here for."

"We're all here for Love? Or you are …?" My voice trails off as I start to think.

They *are* all here for Love. The whole goal of this – this healing, this process, this life – is Love. In every form. In *any* form. And if I love myself, then this is just another way to do that.

"Okay. Let's call him. I'd like to meet him."

I feel lighter. Looser. More hopeful. I'm comfortable with Love now. I'm comfortable with Iris, because she's me. I'm comfortable with Reframing and Unlearning, even if they are a bit intense. I know I'm intense too, which explains why we get along so well. I'm curious to see how the new guy is. I like that we're building a sort of family here in my mind. I like that everyone has a role.

Reframing walks to the door and opens it even as the doorbell chimes.

"When did you fix that?" I ask him, curious about the new, more melodic tone.

"Oh, right around the time Love dropped some redundant weight." He winks at her and steps aside.

I don't know what I was expecting. Something big and burly, maybe? Someone who looks like he can handle the weight of Shame's heavy gloom. Instead, what stands before me is a tall wiry man, in a pristine black suit, with thick glasses perched on his long nose. His hair is parted and impeccable.

I'm kind of disappointed.

Iris, ever so kind, ever so knowing, nudges me gently. "Don't judge what you do not understand."

"You're right. I know you're right."

He walks toward me, his steps measured and deliberate, eyes sweeping over everything. He puts me in the mind of a cop. He reaches his hand out to me, and we shake.

"Thanks for the call." His voice is ripe with authority.

"Thanks for coming," I respond, a little intimidated.

Love surprises me by bounding over to him. Boundaries lifts her off her feet and spins her around. Her head is thrown back on a laugh and he stares up at her with such reverence that I almost feel like an intruder. She smacks a kiss on his mouth, and with her hands on his cheeks careful to avoid mussing his hair, she kisses his forehead, too.

"I'm always so much happier when you're around," she says as she jumps down.

"There's nothing I wouldn't do to protect you," his gravelly voice promises.

Arms twined around one another, they walk toward me with Boundaries matching his pace and gait to Love's. It's impossible to ignore the way he cherishes her. It's even more impossible to ignore how she lets him.

"So," Boundaries asks me. "Mind if you fill me in on the situation while I take a look around?"

"Yeah. Sure. Yes." I'm still intimidated by him, but I can't deny his unmistakable desire to take care of Love.

Out loud, for everyone to hear, Iris says, "He wants to take care of you, too."

Love and Boundaries turn as one to look at me.

"You're uncomfortable again," Love remarks. She comes over to hug me and I feel the radiant jubilation that she is. "It's Boundaries, isn't it?"

I nod, feeling Shame's presence grow bit by bit. "I don't mean to be. I just…"

Boundaries nods, knowingly. "I completely understand. It takes a while to get used to me. Take your time. I'm here to get to know you, so let's just start with the main issue. I think it's pretty obvious judging by the creepy guy standing next to you."

He laughs. I'm staggered by how richly tender it is. Before I can remark, he walks up to Shame.

"Hey man, you gotta go. I can't let you get this close to Love. You know the rules." Boundaries grabs him by the elbow, pulling him toward the door.

"I deserve to be here," Shame protests. He starts talking, but he's getting farther and farther away. I can't make out anything he's saying.

Boundaries hasn't said a word since Shame began making a case for himself. He's just carefully and steadily moving toward the door, making sure Shame is placed on the other side. Boundaries shuts the door, and with a key that he pulls out of his pocket, he locks it.

He comes back to where Love and I are standing with Iris and shakes his head.

"Don't apologize," he says before the apology can form on my lips. "That's what I'm here for. Is it alright if we sit?"

We move to the space that we've used before; sofas that look like the ones that reside in my living room, and a coffee table to match. We sit down, and Boundaries, sitting on the coffee table with a pen and pad, faces me.

"Tell me how I can help you."

I'm a bit surprised by this. Unlearning and Reframing just sort of knew what I needed. Even Love helped me out a lot. But Boundaries is making me lay it all out there for him. My discomfort rises yet again, but before it can get too out of hand, I am imbued with Iris' knowing.

"Emerson," she starts to tell me. "You've done a great deal of work to get here. You have a new foundation. Your mind is a place you are beginning to really enjoy being."

"You're right," I say looking around at the improvements we've made. "It is."

Iris calms my unease, guiding me to look at Boundaries. "It's time to make it a safe space too," she says this as she places my hand over his. "You can trust him."

I feel his hand, firm and sincere. I look into his eyes, and I see Love reflected in them. Trusting Iris, trusting myself, I choose to trust him.

Onto Boundaries I download my entire mental and emotional history. I take him through everything. It takes a really long time, but if he's going to make this mind of mine a safe space, I can't leave anything out.

"And I've just started to accept and relish in Love. I want to protect her. I want to protect me. I don't want to be constantly worried about when Shame is going to show up. I already do that with Grief, and that's the one I know I can't really control. I've come to terms with that," I explain to him. "I really have. I've accepted that Grief and Love are inexorably linked."

Boundaries nods his head as he scribbles down some notes. He gestures for me to continue. I take a deep breath and do just that.

"I need to stop putting other's needs before my own and remember that I am allowed to put my own mental and emotional health first. This is really hard for me, because I've had a lifetime of doing the exact opposite of that. It's been detrimental – not only to my own self, but to my relationships as well. I want to be able to do those things without Shame showing up and telling me that I'm a bad friend or a bad wife. I want to be able to be proud of the things Taggart and I have worked hard for without Should popping in to give me input that I didn't ask for." I sigh here and realize what I really want is to be able to live my life with Love and Iris and Meditation and *their* friends. I trust them. I say as much to Boundaries.

Boundaries reads over his notepad, then lifts his eyes to study my face. We're both silent, absorbing what I've just said. It's not awkward, and the look on his face is full of acceptance.

"I can help. First, you have to understand that just having me here isn't enough. You have to know why I'm here. You have to want me to be here. And as much as I will protect you, you have to protect me."

"I can do that," I assure him.

Iris and Love exchange a look. Love runs a hand down my hair.

"It's harder than it sounds, Emerson. There are a lot of people who don't understand Boundaries. There are even more who like to push him to see how far he can move. You have to hold the line for him. You have to create a safe space for him so that he can create a safe space for you."

Though it sounds daunting, Iris urges me to ask how I do that.

Boundaries and Love are holding hands in front of me. I can feel Iris expand within me just before Boundaries says, "You haven't once addressed me by name since I came in."

Before I can offer a rebuttal, Love steps in. "You haven't, Emerson.

You've thought it, but even in here it's not the same thing. You know there is great power in a name. By using Shame's, you give him meaning. By neglecting to acknowledge Boundaries' you take his away."

My mouth falls open in apology. "I'm sorry. I didn't mean to do that."

All three of them wait. I don't know why it's so hard for me.

"Boundaries isn't a vulgar word," Iris prods me.

So why do I feel like it is? And then I remember.

Weaponized in the name of Love, Boundaries were just one more thing that Loss had taken from me as a child. I flash back to my bedroom door being removed, and how Shame had come with that act. I remember my parents reading my journal out loud and being punished for my private thought and feelings. Shame was there for that, too. I hear myself telling people I don't want to have children; that I've never wanted to have children; and recall with perfect clarity the visits I get from Shames and Shoulds that don't even belong to me. I see myself pleading with God in bookstores and on bathroom floors, to please take the pain of Grief and Loss. By wanting to escape the pain of Grief and the memories of my own family so badly that I begged for days where I wouldn't think of them, I inadvertently called Shame myself.

Iris and Love hold me, lightly rocking me as I look back. As I figure out how to look forward.

"I'm so sorry, Boundaries." I reach out my own arms and pull him into our hold. "I'll protect you. I promise."

We begin our work pretty immediately. I realize my job is not to protect Boundaries from my own mind. He's got that covered. My job, shockingly enough, is to protect Boundaries from everyone else's.

People ask questions. At first, I feel rude not answering. Sometimes they're concerned. Sometimes they're curious. Sometimes they're intrusive. Then I remember; I don't need to earn anyone's Love. I just need to love myself. And protecting Boundaries? That's another way I do that.

It's easy to fall back into old patterns. I want to say yes to everyone. I like seeing the joy on their face. I've learned that even though I don't need to put everyone else first, I do really love helping other people. The only thing I love more than that, is time to myself.

With the help of Boundaries, my mind is becoming a place I enjoy being. A place where I feel safe. I like to retreat into it, to spend time with Love, or Iris, or Meditation. I even read about things I believe and call up Unlearning and Reframing for their perspectives.

Shame isn't allowed to be around Grief anymore. Boundaries, Love, and Iris have taught me that Grief is ever evolving, and that Shame is not a help to anyone's emotional evolution.

I say "No" a lot. *A lot*. In the beginning I'm not good at it, and I offer up explanations that make it sound like I want to say "Yes". I don't actually want to say "Yes" so I end up hurting feelings by harping on the fact that I'm saying "No". I say "No" so much and protect Boundaries too vigilantly. At some point Love has to come in and remind me that Love isn't a wall. Love is a door. Even though it doesn't have to stay open or even unlocked, I can't ignore everyone that knocks on it.

Boundaries likes this explanation. He likes the doorbell that Reframing installed. It sounds even more welcoming than it did before.

"I've taught Shame to use the doorbell. I also put in a peephole, so you'll be able to tell it's him. Feel free to not answer. Though, as ever, the choice is up to you," he reminds me.

"Thanks Boundaries. What about Should?"

"Well, Should has her uses. We've had a talk. She's around when you need her, but she's not allowed to drop in unless it's an emergency."

"I can understand that."

A few days later, I'm on a date with Taggart. We're laughing. We're telling stories. We're having a great time. Something snags at my memory – a scent. A picture. I don't really know. But it brings

Grief to the door. He's emphatic. It's one of those echoing pain visits, the kind I don't see coming anymore. Even though I understand Grief, I'm having a really nice time without him right now. I don't want to let him in.

Grief is ringing the doorbell over and over again, until suddenly he starts to jiggle the knob. Boundaries calls me. He knows Grief is a case-by-case situation.

"Do you want me to let him in?" Boundaries asks.

I don't even have to think about it.

"No."

Boundaries is smiling, I can tell. He smiles every time I say "No."

"I love when people say 'No'. It means they're saying 'yes' to themselves. I've got it under control. Don't worry."

I don't. I trust him.

Forgiveness

There'll be happiness after you
But there was happiness because of you, too
Both of these things can be true
There is happiness
In our history
Across our great divide
There is a glorious sunrise.
– Taylor Swift, Happiness

As dark as things were before is how bright they are now. I don't have the pressure of Shame and Fear bearing down on me, pushing me to be smaller. I know that there are things I can't control, but I also know there are things I can.

My mind is finally a safe space. It's not perfect, but I don't want perfection. I still spend time with Meditation, and we go back and spend time with myselves. I'm always happy to see Younger Emerson now, understanding what I need. Understanding the Love that I know Younger Me doesn't quite know. I sit with myself when I need someone, and even when I think I don't. I just sit there and give myself the Love that one day I will understand. The Love that I don't have to earn. The only Love there is.

I have long talks with Boundaries. I'm so surprised that I was so uncomfortable with him at first because honestly, he's my favorite. I love him so much. I love how he loves Love. How he loves Iris. How he works with Unlearning to understand and refute things I'd hear Percy and his friends say. I never believed them, but I also didn't speak against them. With the help of Unlearning's voracious appetite for information, and Boundaries' understanding of not only myself but others, I do now. We discover a lot about each other, and the closer we get, the more protective I become. It's a good thing. Iris perpetually reminds me how important it is to protect the one that makes you your own safe space.

I don't run to the bathroom and cry anymore. When Grief shows up, I talk to Taggart. I talk to Frankie. I get closer to my longtime friends. I even make new ones; friends who know Grief, friends who have relationships with Depression and Anxiety, friends who have their own Iris. Iris makes friends with their Intuitions, and they talk even when we're not around. It's a beautiful thing. Even though, inevitably, my friends' relationships with their Grief, Depression, Fear, and Loss are different than mine, we understand one another. We empathize with one another. I used to only swim in the shallow end of the emotional pool. Now I'm a deep-sea diver, and I forget that I have legs. I want to trade them for fins and gills.

Fear is still around, but Reframing has helped me understand that as troublesome and contagious as they can be, I need them. Together we work with Boundaries and Fear to understand that there are things I need Fear for. I need them to remind me to follow the speed limit … most of the time. I need them to remind me not to take things for granted. We cover all the things they're allowed to keep files about, and I approve of most of them. Their files are organized and stacked in a decorative manner which is neither looming nor intimidating. Though I never look in the file that talks about the dentist.

Depression still comes to stay. I still have days where I burrow in bed, eating ice cream in my pajamas, binge watching New Girl for the twentieth time. No amount of Prozac or Meditation has rid me of them, but I'm not giving up hope.

Iris has become the Love of my life. I trust her as I have trusted nothing else. It almost feels traitorous to say this since I am so happily, delightfully married to Taggart, but Love has taught me that there are many versions of her. And many ways to express her. Taggart understands that Love doesn't want to compare. He understands about Iris. He's thankful for her. She has become both a place inside me and out of me. I find myself visiting her, bringing Meditation to her as well, instead of the other way around. We have done some miraculous things together and bringing me from the heady emotional Autumn to the refreshing hope of Spring is just the beginning.

I mull all these things over as I watch my own memories float by. It's just me and Iris. Love and Boundaries are always around, taking care of us, taking care of each other. It's beautiful to watch. It's even more breathtaking to feel.

"There's so much more space inside me," I say to Iris. "I can't believe how cramped and outdated this used to be."

She holds my hand as we walk around. I see the corner where I lived with Fear for so long. I see the reel that Shame has carelessly discarded, and bending down to retrieve it, I glance around.

For the first time in a long time, Should comes in. She must've rang the doorbell and I missed it. Boundaries comes in next to her, ready to remove her at the slightest provocation, but Love and Iris know where I'm going.

"Should we watch this?"

Shame isn't making me watch this reel. He's not holding my neck in his signature vice-like grip, feeding me greasy food. There isn't an odor of cigarettes or the smell of burnt popcorn lingering in the air. It smells like Iris and Love and all the things that fill the broken pieces in me. The pieces that I held out to God.

Should doesn't look so perfect now. She's *my* Should. The Should

I know I can ask for advice; the Should I can trust because I know that she has switched sides. She chose the light. And so have I.

"Why do you want to watch it?" She asks this question thoughtfully. She's not looking to poke at me or gang up on me with a bully. Should is a follower and, now that she has better leaders, she's enjoyable most of the time. Besides, I think she has a crush on Boundaries.

"I want to see what it looks like to me now."

Boundaries is cautious. He wants me to be safe.

"Are you sure, Emerson?"

I don't have to check with Iris. Her knowing is my knowing.

"I am."

The doorbell rings, and I smile to myself. I've called the troops, and I've got home court advantage. Since the renovation, I've scoured every nook and cranny of my mind. I've checked out the ceiling, I've had Reframing and Unlearning walk me around with Boundaries and Love so we can understand every single thing in here. It's been educational and enlightening. I'm not afraid to be alone in it. I'm even less afraid to have the Others come in.

Iris is the only one who knows everyone that I've called. And I've called them all.

Loss comes in, confused but intrigued. She's careful to make sure she doesn't touch anything.

Shame comes in after her and Boundaries is stuck to him like glue.

"One wrong move," Boundaries says tightly. "I'm doing this for Emerson. I'm not doing this for you."

"Like I care," Shame shoots back.

Should avoids Shame, sticking close to Love. I thank her, and she nods at me respectfully. Love holds Should's hand.

"Come," she says to her and draws her to a seat far away from Shame.

Depression enters with Anxiety. I always suspected they were close.

Fear doesn't have to come through the door. Fear is always here, but they're much less ominous, much less contagious. I ask them to please be kind and keep to themselves. It takes some coaxing and a stern talking to from Boundaries and Love, but they've agreed.

Grief saunters in from behind the doors. He's piercing today, and it hurts. But I need it to.

Reframing and Unlearning come in together, laughing at some private joke. Reframing sends me his signature wink, and gallantly offers Unlearning his arm.

Meditation sweeps in, the scent of awe trailing behind her like a cape.

"Sorry I'm late everyone!"

"You're not late," I tell her kissing her gleaming cheek. "You look wonderful."

"Thank you," she trills. "I just love what you've done with your mind. No matter how many times I come here, I'm always so inspired."

She gestures over to the seats in front to the movie screen I've set up. "Just sit anywhere?"

"Yes, you're safe."

She taps my nose. "I know."

Everyone is seated, and with Love and Boundaries keeping everyone at bay, I trust that everything will go how it needs to. We've all come to a bit of a detente in the name of curiosity.

I walk to the front, hoping their gazes are all on me. When Iris tells me they are, she goes to door and lets two more in, guiding them silently into the back where they can watch unobtrusively.

She gives me the signal, staying in the back to keep an eye on the newcomers.

"I know you know each other. Just like I know you're not exactly happy about all being here at the same time, sharing space and energy with each other."

Shame sniffs contemptuously. My lips curve as Boundaries pins him with a glare.

"At some point this is going to happen again. And it won't be under these circumstances. So, with that being said," I lift the film cannister that Shame loves the most. The one he left behind.

He perks up. I feel Depression holding Anxiety back.

"I need to watch this. I need to see it on my own terms. With all of you. These are things that happened. You were all a part of all of this, and so it doesn't just belong to him. It belongs to all of you. To all of us."

I ignore the overwhelming mixture of emotions as it begins.

I take my seat in the front, between Love and Meditation, knowing that everyone is watching me. With Iris is in the back, I feel Meditation reach out to me to act as a conduit for Iris and me. I squeeze her hand in thanks as I feel the tethers of Iris rise up in me. Calming me. Centering me. Reminding me why I'm doing this.

It's awful. These memories are terrible and painful, but I see new things.

I see how my mom is holding Charles crying and covering his eyes as Percy throws pots and pans at Keating. I see her mouth moving and realize she's mouthing "I'm so sorry." I see her hug Keating when he comes home from college the weekend he told us he was gay. I see her tell her she loves him. I see her tell him she's always known. I see her apologize for so many things.

I see that Keating screamed "No, Charles get back!" right before my mom snatched Charles out of the way. I see Keating asking my opinion while he shops for clothes for school. I see how Keating let me write my "stories" on his computer and set me up with an email address. He even taught me how to use it to email my writing to myself after the journal incident. I see Keating apologize for hurting me.

I see how Percy bought me a basketball hoop for Christmas one year and would play outside with me for hours when no one else would. I see Percy teaching me about the history of Metallica and Thin Lizzy. I see Percy letting me learn to braid on his long hair. I see Percy wearing a gas mask as he changes Charles' diaper. I see us all laugh until we cry.

I see the Love I finally understand on Charles' face when I'm teaching him about fractions and making him fried chicken for dinner when Mom is working late to make sure we can pay bills. I see him riding a bike without training wheels and screaming with glee. I see him getting dressed in the outfit we chose together for his first homecoming dance. I see him sneaking into my room after everyone is asleep to see if I'm okay. I see the text he sent me after I thanked him for changing my flat tire, telling me that I was his sister, and he would do anything for me.

I see so many moments that are good, that are filled with Love. I see so many moments where we are all pulled in so many directions by so many things.

I see that these people, all of these people, are just humans. They are flawed and imperfect. I know that we are all the villains and the heroes in someone's story. This just happens to be mine.

I watch the reel to the very end. Love jumps up to turn the lights on. I sit quietly in the aftermath. I let all the feelings wash over me. I feel everything at once and I embrace it. This is who I am.

After a bit, I stand to address the space. "I'm going to be talking with each of you. Please respect the privacy and be patient. I promise you; I will give each and every one of you individual attention."

I catch Boundaries' eye and, almost imperceptibly, he nods. I know he understands that he and Love are in charge.

In the space of my mind that I have reserved for private, intense thought, I call in Should.

She takes a seat, but she doesn't really relax. She and I have already talked, but there's something else I want to say to her.

"I want to thank you," I tell her.

She looks a little surprised.

"You didn't see that coming? You should have." We laugh like comrades at this. "But seriously, Should. I really appreciate your evolution. It's been wonderful to watch."

She rises to her feet to leave. When she gets to the door, she turns around.

"It's been wonderful to watch yours too, Emerson."

I feel the tightness in my chest loosen and, at the brisk tap on the door, implore Unlearning to enter.

She steps in and walks right to me. She puts her hands on my face and kisses my forehead.

We talk for a bit. We talk about all that she's helped me with, and how I understand that there will be so much more that I need her for.

"I know that as life goes on, as I continue to age and grow, there will be tons of things I need you for. I don't even know what I don't know, and sometimes I don't know why I believe the things I do. That's where you come in. I really look forward to our time together. You've become one of my favorites."

She blushes. "You're not just a job, Emerson. I care about you."

I watch as her eyelashes grow spiky with tears.

"I love you," she tells me.

"I love you, too."

Reframing comes in after her, lifting me off my feet in his surprisingly powerful arms. "I'm so fecking proud of you, kid!"

Letting him spin me around, we share an ebullient laugh.

"You reshaped my mind," I smile hugely. "You reshaped my life."

"No, I didn't," he responds, blowing his great nose into his handkerchief. "You did that. I just brought the tools."

We talk about the add-ons and the work we have yet to do. We're deep in the fun of construction plans when there's a meek rap at the door.

"Ah, time got away from us," he says rolling up his blueprints and tucking them under his arm. "I'll see you soon. Best get to it."

Depression ambles in. I'm glad I brought in Reframing and Unlearning first. They've steeled me for this conversation.

Depression stands in front of me, hands folded, eyes cast down. I walk to them and lift their eyes to mine.

"You were just trying to help," I say to them. I take their hands in mine.

"I was," they begin. "The Loss, the abuse, the pain – it's too much, Emerson. It's too much."

I hold them as they cry, shedding a few of my own tears with them.

"I know," I say over and over again. "I know."

After a while they gathers themselves. I don't rush them. They're a slow mover.

"I'll see you again soon." Their voice is fully of apology.

"I know," I repeat.

I stare at the door that closes behind them, knowing who's next.

Fear comes in, bold and unapologetic. I've learned to laugh with them, and to appreciate their caution, even if I don't like their tendency to get out of control.

"You wanted to protect me," I say before they can say anything.

"I still do," They admit.

"You will. But you're not in charge anymore. You won't ever be again."

They stare at me stoically. I don't back down. Finally, they get up and go to the door.

"Have it your way."

When Fear leaves, Anxiety comes speeding in.

"Am I late? Oh, I'm so sorry..."

I lift my hand to him. "I know we don't know each other too well, but I'd like to leave it there. I appreciate the attempt, but I have enough on my plate."

Anxiety wrings his hands. "Did I –"

I don't let myself hear the rest. I guide them to the door and usher them out. I make my way back to my chair and sit down. Even after that small amount of time with those three, I'm exhausted.

Grief comes in next, opening the door himself. I chuckle a little.

Grief is always trying to give Boundaries the slip. Seems like it worked this time.

"Hello, Emerson."

He looks like himself. The one who brought the contracts to my house all those years ago.

"You don't have a briefcase?" I ask, teasing him.

"I'm sure I can scrounge one up if you really want. I know how sentimental you are."

I tell him that even though it's perverse, I'm really glad I get to spend the rest of my life with him.

"I like you, too." He says to me.

"I didn't say that," I protest. "I just want you to know that I love you. I love what you're doing for their legacy, even when it hurts. I love the memories that you show me. You remind me just how much of them I have stored in here." I tap my temple. "As long as they're there, they're not gone. So, I guess I'm really saying thank you. So, thank you."

He engulfs me, and we both cry like babies. He is – and will always be – so painfully comfortable. But it fits so well. Because if I didn't need Grief; if they had all lived? How I felt about them would feel a lot like that.

After Grief hulls me out, I call in Love. I need to feel full of something effervescently deep. She comes in like a laugh.

"My darling!" Clutching me to her, she weeps shimmering tears of light. "You have no idea how proud of you. You've done so much work and so much of me is in you." She looks around. "I don't even need to be in here. I'm in you."

I cup her face in my hands and lock eyes with her. "I just needed you. I needed to feel you."

She smiles at me maternally. She takes my hands from her face and puts them on my heart. "So you shall. So you will."

Kissing my lips, she promises that she's not going anywhere.

"I know," I whisper under my breath as the door closes behind her.

Boundaries comes in next, assuring me that everything is under control.

I interrupt him mid-sentence. "I know they are. I trust you. You are so incredibly capable. You know what I need before I even do."

He smiles at me a bit smugly. "It's my job to know you better than you know yourself. How else can I protect you?"

I laugh. "You're quickly becoming my favorite."

"I should be," he retorts with a laugh of his own.

We sit there smiling cheekily at each other.

"I might be a little in love with you."

"It's because I remind you of Taggart," he says. "But I'll take it. And I'll raise you. Drop the 'might'."

We hug and I feel so safe, so secure, so protected. This is what Depression and Fear were trying to do and couldn't. No one else could.

"Thank you," he whispers in my ear. "For being my champion. I know it's not easy."

"Nothing good ever is."

Feeling safely impenetrable, I invite Shame in. I know Boundaries is right outside the door, ready to intervene at a moment's notice.

Shame tries to come toward me, to approach the desk, but I am full of Love and Boundaries. He can't.

"What do you want?" It slides out of him, thick and oily leaving stains on the air.

"I wanted to thank you."

I feel his shock. I'm met with silence.

"You taught me a lot. You showed me a lot. But we're done now. I don't need you. I don't want you. You're not welcome here anymore."

He starts to laugh, that insidious laugh that always makes my skin crawl. It doesn't this time, and it pisses him off.

"I don't want to hate you," I say to him, softly. "I understand you. I really wish I didn't, but I do. I just don't have any use for you anymore."

Before I even look up, Boundaries has opened the door and is dragging Shame out of my mind and into the bright light of reality, where I know he can't survive.

After Shame, I make a choice. I call out to Iris and decide to tackle Loss. She walks in tentatively, somehow charmingly respectful.

She stands in an awkward spot. I can tell she doesn't want to touch anything.

"Please have a seat," I tell her.

She lowers to a chair. "Why am I here? Do you have an assignment for me?"

I sweep my gaze over her. The sadness, the hesitancy. She doesn't like what she is, but she accepts it.

"Loss, I want you to know that I don't blame you."

I hear her sharp intake of breath, but I continue on.

"I'm so sorry that I blamed you. It's not your fault. I know you have a job to do, and that it is a thankless one. I know that you are often blamed for choices that other people make. I understand that. I really, really do."

Her astonished eyes meet mine. "You do?"

I reach out to her, nodding my head when she shakes hers emphatically.

"Please," I beseech her.

"I don't want to take anything from you," her voice trembling.

"I want you to have something. It's a gift, free and clear. No strings attached."

I keep my hand outstretched patiently waiting. After a few minutes, she places hers on mine.

"It's warm. I don't know that anyone's given me this before." Her eyes go dreamy. "What is it?"

"It's Love. Take as much as you need, Loss. I've got plenty."

I thought the conversation with Loss would leave me drained, but it doesn't. It seems the more Love I gave her, the more I had. I don't know if I'll ever fully understand Love, but I'm so thankful for it.

Iris shows up, and we have an unspoken conversation full of

Love, Gratitude and so much light I'm sure I could be seen from universes away. She is not separate from me. I've finally begun to understand that there is no universe in which she is not with me. I love her so deeply that I don't know if there is an actual word for what I feel for her. I intend to do anything to protect her. I tell her all of this, and she radiates through me so brightly that I feel like joy epitomized.

"I will do the same for you," she tells me. "And more."

After our communication, I ask Iris for the ones I've been hiding from everyone. She strokes a hand down my hair and goes to get them.

An ominous knock brings Death to my door.

"Hello, Death. Come on in." Opening the door, I welcome him in.

He walks in slowly, and I shut the door behind him.

"What am I doing here, Emerson?"

"Please have a seat."

He sits on a chair in much the same manner as when I saw him last. He doesn't look his best. His clothes are shabby. His nails are too long. His hair needs washed, and he has holes in his shoes. I pour him a glass of water, which he takes suspiciously.

"What am I doing here, Emerson?" He repeats. He takes his glasses off, rubbing the bridge of his nose wearily. I smile to myself at the familiarity of the gesture.

"I'm not angry with you."

"Well, you're not about to die, either. So will you please tell me what I'm doing here?"

I sit on the coffee table my knees almost touching his. I wait and wait, until he looks up at me. Meeting his eyes, I see they are replete with sorrow and guilt.

I grab his hands before he has a chance to recoil. I hold them in my own, infusing them with Love.

"It's not your fault. None of it is your fault."

His eyes widen in shock.

"I know I blamed you, but I was wrong. You are the one thing in this world that we are all certain of. I was never going to be okay that you showed up. I was never going to be okay with your job. But that has nothing to do with you."

I feel Iris bring someone else into the room.

"Death, you're just doing what you're supposed to do. It has nothing to do with me. It doesn't even have anything to do with the people you take. You know when you're supposed to show up. You don't get a say when or how."

"I don't," he says softly. "I don't want to hurt anyone. I don't want anyone to hurt."

"I know that, too."

I invite the other figure into the room to come forward.

"Look at me." I implore Death.

He does, and the dry emotion in his eyes tells me more than his tears ever could.

"I forgive you."

"Forgive yourself too," the figure says, laying their hands on Death's brittle shoulders. "What you are doing is an act of Love. Whether or not you realize it."

We stay like that for a few moments, holding each other in Forgiveness.

Death's shoulders shake in dry, wracking sobs. The kind where no tears come. He tells us is haunted by the pain he has left in his wake. He apologizes to me over and over and over for all that he's taken from me. And with each apology I tell him I forgive him.

After what feels like days, infused with Love and Forgiveness, Death elegantly rises to his feet. He looks exquisite. Beautiful. Kind. Gracious.

I tell him so.

"Thank you. Everyone sees me differently."

I'm alone with Iris and Forgiveness. There's one thing left to do. Meditation comes in, calm, serene.

"Ready?"

"Yes," I respond.

Iris and I go back. I go back to sit with myself during the darkest moments of my reel.

"I forgive you," I whisper as Calvin cries on the phone. As he stops calling. As he scares me with the intensity of his Love. As he relapses.

"I forgive you," I whisper to my mom as she takes the wooden spoon she is handed. As she tells us Calvin doesn't love us. As she reads my journal. As she cowers in Fear.

"I forgive you," I whisper to Keating as he shoves me down the stairs. As he calls me fat. As he calls me stupid. As he washes drugs down with expensive wine.

"I forgive you," I whisper to Charles as he hides things. As he ignores my phone calls. As he walks away from me. As he doesn't wake up.

"I forgive you," I whisper to Percy as he calls Keating a fairy. As he pulls me away from the room where my dying mother is calling for me. As he spits in my food. As he tells me he loves me. As he lies.

"I forgive you," I whisper to myself as I watch the bruises bloom on Keating. As I see Charles lay immobile in his bed. As I leave my mother calling out for me. As I struggle to return the hug that Calvin has waited eleven years for. As I write that I still love Percy. As I let him go.

I come out of Meditation awash in release.

"I forgive you," I say out loud to myself. As I move forward.

Acknowledgements

No part of this book, or my healing, would be possible without the enduring kindness, belief and support from my husband, Timothy. Thank you, for not only loving all the parts of me, but for bringing the shining beacon of light that you are into my darkness. Being loved by you is like waking up to the wonder of snow on Christmas morning, every morning.

To Sherry who was the first person who ever saw my fear, my shame, and dragged it –and me – into the light. You are my oldest, dearest friend in the world, and no matter where our lives lead us, your constancy is one of the tethers I can always find.

To April, who has brought so much perspective to this book, to this life, that I never thought possible. This book would not be what it is if it weren't for you.

To Jenn, who has never judged me and always loved me for exactly who I am. I didn't think friends like that existed until I met you. I love you more than you will ever know.

To Andrea, who is the epitome of warmth. You are the sister of my heart.

To Allison, who is the voice of reason and kindness. Thank you for your lifetimes of friendship.

To Gabby and Diana, whose truth and love transcend. Thank you. Thank you. Thank you.

To Lauren and Ambrosia whose grace and sight are unparalleled.

To my creative family. Finding you had been the best, most serendipitous form of self-care.

To Dr. Orbison. Thank you for your candor, your insight, and for caring about me even when you didn't have to.

To the family I married into: I love each and every one of you so much more than I could ever express. The past ten years with you have been the best ten years of my life. I am so thankful for your love, your acceptance, and your beautiful, beautiful hearts.

To my foundational family: we weren't perfect, but you were perfect for me. I am so thankful to have been yours, and for you to have been mine. There has been so much happiness because of you, and so much joy. Those are the things I choose to look back on, without pain, because I understand that you loved me the best way you could. I love you all so much more than even I knew. Thank you for your roles in my life. Thank you for everything you did – and for everything you didn't do – because you have made me the woman I am. And I like her.

Lastly, to Iris. Your presence in my life has changed me for the better and the brighter. I am so thankful for and to all that you are, and all that you continue to be. You are the life raft I always reach for. You are my handrail in the middle of the night. You are the muse behind it all.

Made in the USA
Las Vegas, NV
12 February 2022

43836493R00094